ALSO BY RANDY POWELL

Three Clams and an Oyster

Run If You Dare

Tribute to Another Dead Rock Star

The Whistling Toilets

Dean Duffy

Is Kissing a Girl Who Smokes Like Licking an Ashtray?

My Underrated Year

# SWISS MIST

# RANDY POWELL

# SwissMist

FARRAR STRAUS GIROUX

NEW YORK

Copyright © 2008 by Randy Powell

Distributed in Canada by Douglas & McIntyre Ltd.

Printed in the United States of America

Designed by Jonathan Bartlett

First edition, 2008

1   3   5   7   9   10   8   6   4   2

www.fsgkidsbooks.com

Library of Congress Cataloging-in-Publication Data

Powell, Randy.

Swiss mist / Randy Powell.— 1st ed.

p.   cm.

Summary: Follows Milo from fifth grade, when his mother and philosopher
father get divorced, through tenth grade, when his mother has married a wealthy
businessman and Milo is still a bit of a loner, looking for the meaning of life.

ISBN-13: 978-0-374-37356-6

ISBN-10: 0-374-37356-6

[1. Coming of age—Fiction.    2. Divorce—Fiction.    3. Identity—Fiction.
4. Washington (State)—Fiction.]    I. Title.

PZ7.P8778Sw 2008

[Fic]—dc22

2007027680

*For Judy, Eli, and Drew*

# SWISS MIST

# Fifth Grade

# 1

house–roof–cover–shelter–protection–
defense–bastion–wall–division–separation

We lived in Seattle in a small house that had a big back-yard. Right smack in the middle of the backyard was a brick barbecue. In all the years we'd lived there we'd never used the barbecue, but it still had the charcoal smell of all the cookouts from past owners.

"You can roast an entire boar on that barbecue," my dad said. "Those bricks, Milo, see those bricks? They're from the same lot of bricks that were used to build the fire station and the Episcopalian church—the oldest buildings in this neighborhood."

My dad, Luke Bastion, was a philosophy teacher at a small private college. My mom, Cori, volunteered at my school and worked part-time in a candy shop. My parents loved living in Seattle and doing city things like going to plays and concerts, eating out, and looking at old buildings in different neighborhoods.

Dad had a short, well-groomed beard and zinc-colored hair that he combed straight back and tied in a ponytail. Actually, it was more like the tail of a small wet rodent than that of a pony. He had a round bald spot on top of his cranium. He took psychedelic drugs.

"For research," he told me.

Dad was always frank and open with me about his drug use.

"Mind experimentation is part of my job as an educator and seeker of enlightenment," he said. "Unlocking doors of the mind and consciousness; journeying through unknown corridors that connect our human mind with the great cosmic intelligence that controls all of life, from the orderly orbiting of the planets to the hooked beak of the jayhawk."

He shook a big stack of pages at me.

"Look at all these notes I've taken, Milo. My philosophy. Look how tiny my handwriting is! Have you ever seen such tiny handwriting?"

One of my dad's favorite things to do was step out into our backyard at sundown, when the shadows crept between the houses, lean against the brick barbecue puffing his pipe, and gaze musingly at the sky. Or gaze musingly at a blade of grass. Or a bug. Or a brick. Let's face it, he was usually so high in the evenings he would gaze musingly at most things.

Sometimes he'd invite me to step outside with him. I'd inhale the smells of charcoal barbecue, mown grass, burning pipe tobacco, and neighborhood chimney smoke.

You could argue that Dad and I didn't have a whole lot in common. He had a bald spot and I didn't. He smoked a pipe and I didn't. He used hallucinogenic drugs and I didn't. He was deep. I was shallow: all I wanted was a BMX bike for my birthday.

But as my dad told me many times, we had one very important thing in common.

"We're both on a quest for truth," he said. "You may not realize it yet, Milo, but you will. Right now your brain is still operating on the concrete-literal level. But the time will come when you're ready for the higher concepts, and I'll be able to share my complete philosophy with you—I should have it pretty well worked out by then. I guess that's about all I have to offer you—I can't teach you how to catch a ball or hammer a nail, but I can teach you how to seek the truth."

It gave me a good feeling to know that someday I would know what he was talking about.

"In the meantime," he said, "it would probably be best if you didn't emulate some of my more questionable practices."

"Huh?" I said.

"Don't do what I do," he said. "And work on building your vocabulary. If you're going to be ready to receive the concepts I share with you, you'll need a firm grasp of your mother tongue."

Mom was the one who taught me how to catch a ball and hammer a nail. She also helped me with my homework and took me to dentist appointments, Scout meetings, and baseball practice. When I was a little kid, she pitched me imaginary baseballs in the backyard. I'd hit them over the fence and the fire station and the Episcopalian church. When I got older, we played catch with a real ball and she threw me grounders and fly balls. We threw the football around. She taught me how to block and tackle and come charging out of a three-point stance. She was a coach's daughter. Her dad, my grandpa, had been the great Romney Nordquist, one of the Four Norsemen of Ballard High School football legend, who went on to coach the North Pilchuck High School Coots for thirty years. He died of a heart attack when I was eight. A coot is a type of duck.

Mom would try to drag Dad out in the backyard with us. "Come on, old man, we need a catcher" (or outfielder, or ball shagger). "Come on, Luke, shake your booty."

Dad was afraid of low-flying insects. He was also afraid of colliding with the brick barbecue. Mom, who had collided with it many times, said that our yard would be much safer and roomier if it didn't have that brick thing smack in the middle of the nice green lawn and this year, dammit, before Milo finishes fifth grade, we are going to take it apart brick by brick and haul the bricks to the dump. Nonsense, you'll do no such thing, that's a perfectly functional barbecue and I intend to use it for grilling steaks this summer. Sorry, old man, it's coming down. Oh no it isn't. Oh yes it is—and what are you talking about grilling steaks, you don't even eat meat. Yes I do. Bull, you're a vegetarian! I am not!

My fifth-grade year, they didn't just fight about the barbecue, they fought about money, household chores, Dad's drugs. They were sinking deeper and deeper into debt. House payments, car payments, drug payments—bills, bills, bills. Dad had invested their savings into a get-rich-quick scheme, and lost it all.

I can't think of too many things worse than lying in my bed at night and hearing my parents screaming at each other.

On April 5, the morning of my eleventh birthday, Mom and Dad blindfolded me, then led me out to the backyard and took off the blindfold and pointed to my birthday present, which was leaning against the brick barbecue: a brand-new, fully assembled BMX bike. The kind with high handlebars, an elongated seat, and fat bouncy tires specially designed for doing jumps and stunts on trails. Never had I felt such pure joy and jubilation. I ran around the yard cheering. Then I got on the bike and rode it all day and made it part of me.

A couple weeks after that, on a Sunday morning, my parents were nose-to-nose in the living room having a great big fight. I happened to pass by in search of my batting gloves just as my dad was giving my mom a shove, causing her to fall backward onto the coffee table and break it. My mom just sat there for a moment. I had no word in my vocabulary for the look on her face. I found my batting gloves and went to practice. All during practice I kept seeing the look on her face. By the time practice ended and I got home, Dad had packed a couple bags and moved out.

# 2

nervousness–stress–anxiety–strain–
effort–labor–work–job–profession–teacher

I went to school every day with a nervous, bunched-up stomach. I felt sorry for both of my parents, but especially for my dad, because he was the one who had moved away. He was crashing in his friend Wally Katola's basement. I didn't see much of him during that time, because he was trying to get his life straightened out. I'd overheard my mom's older sister, Shan, say that she'd heard he was in some sort of trouble in his job at the college. Every time I thought of something ordinary such as my dad's bald spot or the smell of his shirt, it felt like my heart was breaking. And then I would take those feelings and stuff them back into me, like I was loading gunpowder down a musket barrel.

I don't think I would have made it through that spring if it hadn't been for my fifth-grade teacher. Ms. Swinford was strict and she made us work hard, but she was always up and bubbly. She had short curly hair, plump apple-red cheeks, red lipstick, and light blue cat's-eye glasses with sparkly jewels embedded in the frames. She told us stories about her childhood growing up on a farm in Wenatchee in eastern Washington. I loved hearing about her big happy family—her parents, sisters, brothers, cousins, dogs, cats. All that happiness! We learned more about Wenatchee than we'd ever need to know. She did that with all sorts of subjects, made us go deep into them and care about them as if we owned them.

Her favorite subject in the world was Switzerland.

When she was twenty she'd spent a year living in Switzerland with Aunt Liesl and Uncle Cedric, who owned a genuine Swiss chalet. Ms. Swinford had a whole Power-Point slide show she'd made about her trip. And a shelf full of books about Switzerland, all with big glossy color photos of the Matterhorn and the villages and cities and farmers and children. It made me so happy to look at those pictures of Switzerland; it felt like I belonged in the meadows of wildflowers and the Swiss villages. Just the word *Alpine* gave me tingles. As a mountain, the Matterhorn ruled.

Matterhorn!

Aunt Liesl and Uncle Cedric weren't her real aunt and uncle, but you could tell she really loved them. They had a view of the Matterhorn from their back porch. They had climbed many surrounding mountains. She showed us pictures of them. Uncle Cedric had a pencil-thin mustache and a felt hat like the Swiss men wear. Aunt Liesl had thick blond braids coiled around her head, like ram horns.

Ms. Swinford also used to tell us she had a little friend named Virginia who lived inside the cuckoo clock with the cuckoo. It was a genuine made-in-Switzerland cuckoo clock and the cuckoo would come out at the stroke of every hour, but Virginia was too shy to come out, even when we were "good citizens."

I didn't really believe there was somebody named Virginia living inside the cuckoo clock, but part of my mind did, because back then, back in fifth grade, I was able to believe in just about anything.

A handful of us fifth graders would sometimes stay in the classroom during lunch or recess and listen to Ms. Swinford's Swiss music. We'd talk about Switzerland and movies and ghosts and Bigfoot and UFOs and a hundred other things.

"You all have a purpose in life," Ms. Swinford would say. "A grand purpose and destiny just waiting to be discovered. Just remember, something good is always waiting for you at the next turn; everything is a part of the perfect plan of the universe. Spread sunshine wherever you go."

The biggest teacher's pet was a girl named Penny Partnow. She was the tallest, smartest, most mature, most talented person in the fifth grade, and she never let any of us forget it. I hated her, partly because she was so good at everything, but mostly because she had a big mouth.

"I know exactly what *my* purpose and destiny are," Penny said. "I'm going to travel the world, then be an actress, and then retire from acting and get elected President."

"Of what?" I said. "The Know-It-Alls of America?"

I was the only one of my friends brave enough to insult Penny to her face. She took karate and could have easily torn any of us apart both verbally and physically, but she always left me alone because it was kind of common knowledge that Penny liked me. I had no idea why she liked me, but I took advantage of it.

"I wonder where we'll all be five years from now," Ms. Swinford said. "Just think, five years from now you boys and girls will be in tenth grade! High school sophomores!"

"Unless I decide to skip a couple of grades," Penny said. "Which I may do."

"Who else knows what his or her purpose and destiny are going to be?" Ms. Swinford asked. "How about you, Milo?"

"How should I know?" I said. "I'm only a fifth grader."

"What about you, Ms. Swinford?" somebody asked.

"My destiny? Oh, I'm living mine, right here and now. This is where I'm meant to be."

• • •

One sunny morning in May about a month after my dad had moved out, Ms. Swinford had the class singing "The

Happy Wanderer." I was feeling especially sentimental and heavy-hearted that morning, and for some reason that song really got to me. All sorts of memories and feelings just flooded in. The smell of my dad's shirt, the sight of Dad leaning against the brick barbecue in the quiet evening, Mom tossing him a ball underhand so he could catch it.

When we got to the part that goes "I wave my hat to all I meet, and they wave back to me," I felt myself losing it. I thought of a little boy, just like myself, a knapsack on his back, walking along the trail, waving his hat to all the other happy hikers and getting waved back to by them. All the pain and stress I'd been stuffing down for the past month or so started fizzing up, right there in class. I could feel it coming and I knew I was going to start crying. I had to get out of the room. I got up and made for the door just as the first big sob hit me. Penny Partnow was sitting in the front row and as I rushed past, our eyes locked for a second, and I noticed something in her expression, something gentle. Then I continued out of the room.

When I got to the hallway, I sat down on the floor with my back against the wall and started crying.

Ms. Swinford came out. "Milo? Are you okay?"

"My . . . my stomach. I guess it's something I ate."

"Do you need to go to the nurse's office?"

I shook my head.

Ms. Swinford knelt down and put her hand on my forehead. That day she was wearing some kind of sleeveless button-down blouse. Her bare arms were fleshy and feminine. She smelled fresh and outdoorsy, like the sky. Like Wenatchee or the Swiss Alps.

"Here, come with me," she said.

She led me to a door at the end of the hall. She unlocked the door and flipped on the light. It was a narrow room with a black couch and a bookcase against the wall. She said it was a "quiet room" for teachers who needed to get away for a moment of peace.

She handed me some tissues. "Here you go, wipe your face. Why don't you sit down."

I sat and breathed in the tissues. They smelled outdoorsy, too.

"I guess you feel pretty awful, huh?" she said. She looked around the room and bit her lower lip, the way she often did when she was about to tell us one of her stories about Switzerland. "You know what I do sometimes when I feel really bad?"

"What?"

"I sit very still and listen for a minute. As hard as I can. You know what I listen to? Well, sometimes the bad feeling is trying to tell me something . . ."

She bit her lip again and looked around the room some more.

"And, um, sometimes I open a book." She reached down to the bookcase where there were maybe five or six dusty books on the shelf. "Ah, here's a book of synonyms. You remember what synonyms are, right? Words that mean the same thing. So what I do is I play a little game. The synonym game. I ask myself, 'Okay, what do I feel right now?' What do you feel? Awful? Bad?"

"My stomach feels sick," I said.

"All right, *sick*. Let's look up *sick* in our synonym book. Here we go, see? *Deranged, disabled, not up to snuff. Sickness: complaint, disease, disorder, illness, nausea, vomiting* . . . Hm, well, this game sucks." She snapped the book shut.

I laughed. I didn't feel any better—but I kind of liked the game.

# 3

baseball team–gang–company–friend–
ally–link–chain–leash

The rest of that spring I poured all my concentration
into baseball and Cub Scouts.

We had a great neighborhood baseball team. It was like
a big blended family. The parents of my teammates were
all nice and they seemed to have no marital problems.
During games they'd fill up the stands for a big parentfest.
Our three coaches were model dads who kissed their wives
in public and gave a huge amount of their lives to our baseball team. One of the coaches was also my Cub Scout
leader.

Mom was pretty depressed but she still made it to every
game and Cub Scout event.

I didn't see Dad until after school ended when he came

and got the last of his stuff from the house. I helped him load the boxes into his car. Then he took me to lunch downtown in Pioneer Square.

He ordered a veggie sandwich and a bowl of tomato soup.

He had gotten braces.

"I'd always been meaning to," he said. "Get my teeth straightened and the gaps filled and improve my smile. And I have some more good news. I'm moving out of Wally's basement."

"That's great," I said, and I really meant it. "Where are you moving to?"

"Oh, I have a couple of different options. I'm going to do a bit of traveling for a while. I don't feel guilty about getting all this dental work done at this stage of my life," he said, showing me his new braces again. "I get them off in nine months. So . . . are you looking forward to sixth grade next year?"

"Yeah, I guess."

He nodded. He always looked very serious and professorly, especially with that finely trimmed beard. But that day I noticed the hairs of his eyebrows were sticking up all deranged. He didn't have Mom to pluck and groom them while he lay his head on her lap.

"Look, Milo, you're not entertaining hopes that your mother and I will ever get back together, are you?"

I stared at him dumbly. *Of course* I was entertaining hopes.

"Being married to the same person all your life is like having the same philosophy all your life," he said. "Or eating the same lunch every day or working at the same job. These notions of permanence and monogamy are fine for some people, but who says that's the one true way? Why are people so afraid of change? We ought to embrace change."

Dad slurped the last spoonful of his soup, careful not to drip any on his beard. Then he took his soup spoon and started wiping it off with his napkin.

"I want to tell you something very important, Milo. You are the protagonist of your own life story. Don't blame other people for the way you turn out, and don't walk around seeing yourself as a victim of anything. It's all just a story, our own big Hollywood drama. We feel guilty because we don't like how the story is going, so we look around for somebody else to blame for it."

I nodded at what he was saying. It sounded important, but I didn't really understand it. Did it have something to do with why he'd gotten braces? Or why he'd pushed Mom onto the coffee table?

"By the way," Dad said, "I'd like to clear up some misconceptions that may or may not have been planted in your mind—probably by your lovely and charming aunt Shan."

He explained that he had been asked to resign from the college. They said his teaching performance had dropped below standard. "Of course, it didn't help that I had a dalliance with a student," he said.

I wasn't sure what that word meant, but it struck me as a beautiful word.

"Gina—the student I was involved with—was very mature. A senior, but so wise, wise beyond her years. I didn't have to resign, but they wanted to get rid of me. So they offered me a nice little chunk of money, what's called a *severance package*, and I took it straight to the orthodontist. It was time for me to go; I was a good teacher, but it was all just a game, and I'm done with that particular phase, done with teaching. I'm ready for a new game."

"But what about all your research?" I asked him. "Your notes on your philosophy."

"I couldn't read my damn handwriting," he said. "Besides, it's all wrong, none of it makes sense anymore. I was in a different state of consciousness then. I've thrown it out. I'm working out a new philosophy now, a new path."

Dad ran his hand over the top of his head and down his ponytail.

"We have to stay fluid, Milo. Marriage was interesting, but that particular phase of my life is over for me and it's time I moved on. It doesn't mean the marriage wasn't a success."

"What'll you do?"

"Continue my journey. The journey of self-discovery and truth-seeking."

"Will I ever see you?" I felt a clot forming in my throat.

"Right now I'm not exactly certain where I'll be hanging my hat. That's the way it's got to be if you're a seeker and a free spirit. You have to trust the path. The path knows where it's going. These are words you're old enough to understand, Milo: Our paths, yours and mine, are heading in the same direction, but they're not parallel. They twist and turn, and they'll always keep intersecting, whenever the time is right."

"But, Dad, how are you going to live? What are you going to do for money and food and all that?"

Dad held up his spoon and looked at it very intently. He seemed to be waiting for an answer to come from the spoon. Then I realized he hadn't heard my question. He was using the spoon to check out his braces.

After Dad dropped me off at home, I told my mom all about our lunch. One part in particular made her go into a fit of hysterical laughter. Then she abruptly stopped laughing, and her expression went blank and the color drained out of her face. She spent the rest of the weekend walking around the house dressed in tattered sweatpants and a T-shirt, eating handfuls of Lucky Charms out of the box and muttering, "It doesn't mean the marriage wasn't a success . . . It doesn't mean the marriage wasn't a success . . ."

# 4

bills–debt–in the hole–depression–pit–
mine shaft–lode–gold mine–resource–lexicon

Aunt Shan came over quite a bit, sometimes to cook a meal or tidy up the house or go through a stack of bills. Grandma Nordquist came when she could, but she lived fifty miles away in North Pilchuck. There was much talk about lawyers and child support and "he goes and gets goddamn braces on his teeth at this time in his life when he doesn't even have a job . . ."

Mom was really going downhill. She seemed to have given up. She stayed in bed or on the couch, popping pills and drinking wine and sounding groggy day in and day out, eating jelly beans and Junior Mints. Shan and Grandma made Mom flush her pills down the toilet. They paid for a life coach. Meetings were held, plans were made for how Mom was going to dig herself out of debt and get a decent job.

I still held out hope that Dad would change his mind and come back. It was possible. I checked the mail and phone messages. I kept a lookout for Dad to pull up in front of the house in his car and go straight to the backyard and lean against the barbecue.

Aunt Shan took me aside. "Look, sweetie, I don't want to burst your bubble, but your father is history. He's not coming back. You need to get used to that. Luke Bastion has gone riding off into his own sunset. I'm telling you this because you need to think about your mother. You need to be strong for her. *You'll have to be the man of the house now.*"

I'd heard that saying enough times in movies and on TV to know how useless it was. It reminded me of a boy on the homestead wearing suspenders and fighting off Indians from the upstairs window with Pa's shotgun.

Even though I missed my dad, I kept busy. My Cub Scout buddies and I had graduated from Webelos and crossed over into Boy Scouts, and as Tenderfoots we were working together on our various merit badges.

I also really missed Ms. Swinford. Her gentle presence and cheerfulness would have lifted me out of my doldrums. I was nervous about starting middle school in the fall, but at least I'd be facing it with all my familiar friends from school, Little League, and Cub Scouts. And I could always go back to my elementary school and visit Ms.

Swinford every once in a while if I needed to. Just knowing she was there would really bolster me.

But then in August Mom sat me down and said she had something to tell me. She started crying.

She said her life coach had helped her come up with a plan. She had enrolled in the dental technology program at Kangley Vocational-Technical College. She was going to learn how to become a certified dental technician.

She said we were going to sell the house and move to Kangley. We were going to live in Kangley for the next three years while she completed the program. When she got her certificate, she could get a good job and we could maybe move back to Seattle. But we couldn't afford to live in Seattle now, it was way too expensive, even with Dad's child care payments. If we sold the house she could use her half of the money to pay off the credit card debts and pay for tuition and rent an apartment. In Kangley.

*Kangley*. I couldn't believe it. We couldn't leave Seattle. We couldn't.

Mom was watching me like she was afraid I was going to go berserk and start slamming myself against the wall. And I was on the brink of doing it. I felt sick. I wanted to throw a tantrum and break things. Break furniture. I kept hearing Aunt Shan's words about having to be strong for Mom. Those stupid, useless words. Stupid TV-and-movie crap.

We sold the house by the end of August. We had a yard sale, packed up what was left, and cleaned out the house with the help of friends and a neighborhood work party. Everyone brought food, and it turned into a big potluck / going-away party in our backyard. Somebody brought a portable gas grill for the hot dogs and hamburgers; the barbecue with the ancient bricks sat by itself like an uninvited guest.

I knew it was the last time I'd see my friends for a long time. I felt like they were the last friends I'd ever have. My Scouting friends, my sports friends, my school friends—I could not even imagine starting over again and making a whole new set of friends. We spent most of the party in the backyard pounding each other with cardboard tubes. When we were finished doing that, we lolled around on the grass in the shade. That's when Penny Partnow made her big entrance.

She was with her mother, Cobra Cheswick. Cobra and my mom had become friends while volunteering at the school. They used to take morning walks around Green Lake. I'd heard my mom tell my dad that they lived in a big old house with a bunch of other families they called "domestic living partners."

We all gawked at Penny. She wore large round yellow sunglasses and a yellow dress that *had no straps to hold it up*. What was holding it up? Her black hair was primped and ringletted like a Vegas showgirl's.

She spotted me and immediately came over. Even in that dress, she somehow managed to sit down beside me on the grass.

Not bothering to remove her sunglasses, she started telling me how sad she was that I was moving away, and how she was going to miss me but had all these interesting things lined up that she was going to be doing when school started.

I felt embarrassed by the whole situation. Penny sitting next to me on the grass in that dress, my friends watching. I decided to put on a show.

"Do you live in a commune?" I asked.

"What? You know where I live."

"Is it a commune?"

"Cobra and I share a house with other families."

"That would make it a commune," I said.

Penny sighed. I couldn't see her eyes behind her sunglasses, but she was probably rolling them. "We're a group of people who have things in common. We share most things, including a house. We're not a traditional family— but we're still a family."

"That's more like a tribe," I said. "Do you have a chief?" Some of my friends started snickering. I knew I was being mean, but I couldn't help it. It was my last act in this backyard. My last chance to show off in front of my friends. It didn't feel good, not a bit.

"No, we don't have a chief," she said. "I didn't know you were so interested in my living situation. I would have invited you over."

"What for?"

Just then, Ms. Swinford came into the backyard through

the kitchen. She was dressed in flowing garments, like a goddess. She wore her usual red lipstick and glittery cat's-eye glasses. I didn't even know my mom had invited her.

I got up and left Penny and went over to Ms. Swinford. For a moment I thought she was going to give me a hug. She seemed to hesitate and then she just put a hand lightly on my shoulder. There were beads of perspiration at her temples. She handed me a going-away gift. I tore off the wrapping paper.

Penny had followed me, and when she saw what the gift was she gasped and said, "Oh! What an utterly awesome gift, Ms. Swinford."

"I almost gave you one of my books on Switzerland," Ms. Swinford said.

"How cool, you were going to give *me* a gift?"

"No, Penny, I'm actually talking to Milo right now. So, Milo, I decided on this instead. I hope you're not disappointed."

It was a book of synonyms. No, I was not disappointed. I was in shock that Ms. Swinford had come and had even bothered to give me a gift at all.

"I wrote you an inscription inside," she said.

"I'll read it!" Penny said.

Blocking Penny with my elbow, I turned to the inscription. As I read it, my eyes started to get misty. I didn't want anyone to think I was crying, so I had to toughen up and get control of myself by thinking of something shiny and cold, like my dad's braces.

Here's what Ms. Swinford had written:

> Few things in life are more important than clear and accurate expression of our language. And nothing is more essential to that expression than the ability to distinguish between words of similar meaning. Always choose the most precise word and this will give both illumination and delight to your hearer or reader.
>
> Wishing you the best of luck in your new home,
> Valerie Swinford

The next morning we moved. As Mom and I were driving away from the house, I tried not to let myself get all sad and weepy. I tried not to be *maudlin* (a word I had found in my new synonym book). I tried not to say goodbye to inanimate objects. I thought of that morning Mom and Dad had led me blindfolded to where my new BMX bike was waiting all shiny and bright, right off the showroom floor.

I only said goodbye to one inanimate object: the brick barbecue.

# Sixth Grade

# 5

## city–complex–collection–hodgepodge–maze–tangle–woods–jungle–wild–dog-eat-dog

Kangley was thirty-five miles southeast of Seattle, a city of taverns, bowling alleys, strip malls, thrift shops, and sprawling apartment complexes. Mom got a part-time job as a salesperson in a bathroom accessories shop in one of the nearby strip malls, and she started her first semester at Kangley Voc-Tech.

The apartment complex we moved into was called the Bon Repos, Phase 2. *Bon repos* means "good rest" in French.

Phases 1 and 2 were made up of twelve two-story rectangular buildings, identified by the letters A through L. The buildings were all arranged in a geometrically haphazard pattern. The buildings were connected by cement walkways. We lived on the second floor of Building C. Our balcony looked out on some woods across the parking lot.

"Not my idea of home, but it's close to both our schools," Mom said. "I guess we need to learn that change is just a part of life, don't we? And sometimes that sucks."

I tried to think of what Ms. Swinford might say in this situation.

"This place doesn't seem that bad," I said. "It has a pool and cabana. And woods—with trails."

"I hope I haven't made a terrible mistake," Mom said. "It seemed like a good plan, but you know what? Nothing ever really works out the way you want it to. Something's always waiting up ahead to get you."

• • •

I hadn't seen my dad since our lunch together, but he'd called a couple of times just to let us know he was still alive. He was always vague about where he was and what he was doing except that he was "fully engaged on a new path." It was pretty amazing, really: he had somehow figured out the secret to shedding his old self and reinventing himself. I wasn't angry at him or anything; I was actually sort of in awe that he could start a new life so easily. I just didn't have it in me to do that—let go of the past and turn myself into a new person and get a new bunch of friends. Maybe my dad would show me how to do it when the time was right, when he shared his philosophy with me.

At the start of middle school I signed up for Little League football and transferred into the Kangley Boy Scout troop.

I wasn't sure I wanted to play football, but I had to at least give it a try. After all, I was the grandson of one of the Four Norsemen.

And Mom really wanted me to stick with Boy Scouts, not just for the knot-tying and crafts and outdoor stuff, but for the "positive male role models." It scared the heck out of her that I was entering middle school, where so many kids go in all sweet and innocent and come out juvenile delinquents.

"You are on the ragged fringes of adulthood," she said while she was clipping my toenails. We'd just gotten home from a shopping trip where she'd bought me new football shoes, a mouth protector, and an athletic cup. She was barely out of debt but she wanted me to have the best sports equipment. Always the coach's daughter.

"I'm going to get you through middle school in one piece," she said. "So here's what you have to do for the next three years. These are your jobs." She started wiggling each one of my toes, only instead of saying "this little piggie" she said: "Stay out of trouble. Don't pick up any bad habits. Do your schoolwork. Stay in sports. Stay in Boy Scouts. Five toes and five jobs. And *my* job is to get myself through the dental tech program. If we can just stay focused on our jobs, we'll survive this."

• • •

Kangley Middle School was a big place with very little going for it. It seemed like all my teachers were old and sour, and when they found out I was from Seattle, they looked disgusted and made cracks about how liberal it was.

Kangley was such a gigantic school, it was pretty easy to get swallowed up. Quite a difference from my last school. In Ms. Swinford's class, I'd always felt like my personality shone. Everybody knew me and I knew everybody, and I'd felt like I was sort of *appreciated*. But at Kangley I was back to square one. I didn't want to have to work to prove myself all over again. I would just keep a low profile and blend in. School would be something I'd just get through every day. I'd always heard there'd be a huge difference between elementary school and middle school, and it was true. I missed my old friends and my old life. I didn't want any new ones. Everything here was temporary—it would all end soon enough.

That was true for the Bon Repos apartment complex, too—everything was temporary, the residents most of all. Everybody seemed on their way to somewhere else, climbing the great big ladder of America. There were young married couples with babies. There were elderly folks waiting for the biggest move of all, death. And there were lots of single mothers like my mom, trying to make a new start.

The woods that we could see from our balcony had trails coursing all through them. It was a BMX paradise, with all kinds of jumps, hills, dips, valleys, roller-coaster ups and downs and twists and turns. The woods were just as temporary as everything else around there: they were targeted to be developed into the Bon Repos Phase 3 and Phase 4.

At night, you could stand out on your balcony and hear crickets, frogs, and an occasional owl or coyote. You could also hear idiots dumping their garbage in the woods.

Somehow, without even trying, I made a friend at the apartments. His name was Jastin Spitters. He had dark skin and dark crinkly hair, but I don't know what nationality he was. He could have been part Ethiopian or Sudanese, but he also could have been from Honduras or Jamaica or Samoa. I had no idea. His most distinctive feature was his thick eyebrows: they formed two big arches. They made him look like he was always surprised and delighted.

Jastin and I were in the same grade, and sometimes we rode our bikes to school together, but we really didn't socialize with each other there. We never talked about it, but I guess he had the same attitude about school as I did: stay under the radar and get through the day.

After school, we would ride our bikes on the trails, fly over the jumps, tear around the banked S-turns, between trees, over roots and fallen logs, kicking up dust or splattering mud. You had to watch out for the occasional sofa or junked car or mattress or refrigerator, but that made the trail riding all the more hazardous and exciting.

There were some older boys who had motorbikes. I decided I was going to talk my mom into getting me one.

Not this year, but maybe in seventh grade, for my thir-teenth birthday.

• • •

Mom didn't seem too excited about the false teeth and porcelain dentures she was learning how to make in the dental tech program. She constantly worried that she'd made the wrong decision, but it was too late to change her mind, she said, she was in too deep, there was no turning back, it was going to have to be her chosen career.

"Your father was good in situations like this," she told me. "He used to say, 'There's no better path than the one you're on.' But I don't have that kind of faith."

Occasionally I'd hear her having a discussion with Aunt Shan or Grandma Nordquist or one of her friends on the phone, usually on a Sunday evening. Sometimes in tears, she'd say things like:

"I've got to hold it together . . . I don't think I can do it, I just don't think I can hold it together . . ."

"I have to get us through the next three years . . ."

"I just want to have a little bit of happiness in this life. Is that so much to ask? Just a little bit of happiness?"

Since Mom was having such a rough time, I kept re-minding myself of my five toes: stay out of trouble, don't pick up any bad habits, do my schoolwork, go to all the Boy Scout meetings, play whatever sport happened to be in season.

My whole year was mapped out, just like Mom's: when football ended I would do basketball, and when that ended, baseball.

I ended up liking football because I could just turn my brain off and hit people. I was good on defense—all that tackling practice Mom had given me in our backyard really paid off.

● ● ●

There were a lot of wild kids at the Bon Repos. Probably because so many of the grownups were either away at work or busy taking care of the babies. It seemed like the kids all roamed free. There were plenty who sold drugs and hung out at the cabana. You had to watch who you crossed paths with. There was always somebody looking for a fight. If you looked at the wrong kid the wrong way, he'd just as soon play hopscotch on your face. It didn't take me long to learn how to survive at the Bon Repos: never stare at anybody in a challenging way, and never show any fear.

It also didn't hurt to be friends with Jastin Spitters. He had a mad dog of an older brother who looked out for him.

"I don't know if I want you hanging around with that Jastin boy," Mom said. "I don't know if I trust him. He doesn't seem very honest to me."

Mom's instincts were pretty right. Jastin was a thief. He stole mail. He'd ride his bike to distant neighborhoods and steal mail from mailboxes and sell it to older kids, who in turn sold it to a ring of professional identity thieves. He always had a lot of cash on him. I knew he was marked for jail—it was just a matter of time before he got caught. But he never tried to get me to steal mail with him. He was my BMX buddy. I showed him how to take jumps and land on his front tire, and he watched my back.

# 6

balcony–platform–stage–arena–
theater–battlefield–no-man's-land

"I wish we could escape this place," Mom said.

We were sitting out on the narrow balcony on a warm evening in May.

"What place?"

"These apartments. This god-awful *Kangley*. I miss the city. I miss our old house. Do you miss our old house?"

I didn't know how Mom wanted me to answer that. We'd been living here nine months. I had turned twelve last month. Sure, there were things I still missed. My dad. My friends. Ms. Swinford. Her classroom. Her stories and pictures of Switzerland and Wenatchee. Sometimes I even missed Penny Partnow. But I knew if I told Mom all that, it would make her feel guilty, so I just said, "I don't mind it here. I don't mind the apartments."

"Well, we're stuck here until I finish the program," she said.

"I know that," I said.

She studied me for a second. "How come you don't have any friends at school?"

"I have friends at school."

"Who? Name a couple."

"Why should I?"

"You don't have any school friends."

"So?"

"So I worry about that. You used to have so many friends. I know it's hard to adjust. I know it's hard work to make new friends. It takes effort. You never had to work at it, but now you do."

"I have Jastin."

"Yeah, but all you do is ride bikes."

"What are we supposed to do, have tea?"

"Just watch out. There are too many ways a boy can take a wrong turn around this place. Promise me you won't take a wrong turn, Milo."

• • •

I got a letter from Penny Partnow. It was really long. Four pages, typed. The back of the envelope was sealed with a colorful sticker with wacky writing that said, "I'd chew your gum any day!!!"

The four pages were mostly about her great achievements, but there was a little bit about what life was like in middle school—the school I would have gone to. It sounded a whole lot better than Kangley. At the end of the letter, she really piled it on. First it said, "I miss you." Then, "Gotta go now, please write. LOVE, Penny." And then: "P.S. Let me know if you ever get your e-mail hooked back up and then we can talk online and not by snail mail. Lotsa LOVE. PLEASE WRITE BACK!!!! OR GIVE ME A CALL!!! LOVE, Penny."

I read the letter over again. I had to sit down and collect myself. I felt all shaken up and I didn't know why. I pictured Penny's face. I pictured the way she had looked sitting in her front-row desk. I tried to remember why I had hated her. Probably because she liked me. That was reason enough. Plus, she was obnoxious. Still, she had written me a four-page letter. She was the only one from my old school who had written me, and that was because she liked me and had good writing skills. But she had used the word *love* three times.

I wondered whether I should write back to her. What would the fallout be? I got a pen and paper. I didn't really want to write "Dear Penny" at the top of it. That seemed too intimate. I wanted to ask her if she'd been back to visit Ms. Swinford. I knew she must have, being Ms. Swinford's biggest pet. But I couldn't think of any introductory remarks to write before that.

Why did it take so much effort to have friendships? Maybe that's why I hadn't heard from my dad since Christmas, because it was a lot of hassle and effort. Even getting hold of someone by phone was hard work. Harder than it sounds.

I put the pen down and decided I would wait until I got a burst of energy to write her back.

A couple days later, my mom told me she'd heard some "interesting news" from Cobra Cheswick.

"What? You talked to Penny's mom? Why would you do that?"

"We're friends. We keep in touch."

"How can you still be friends? We don't even live near them anymore."

"Well, you see, there's this thing called the telephone."

"So it's about Penny? That's the news?"

"I didn't say it was about Penny. It's about your teacher, Ms. Swinford. They fired her."

I stared at Mom.

"Apparently," Mom said, "there were complaints. Something about— Are you okay?"

I wasn't okay.

I felt awful for Ms. Swinford. I felt sick.

What had she ever done wrong? Shared her life with us? Shared her love and music and stories? How could they have fired Ms. Swinford? She loved teaching. It was her life.

"What'll she do?" I finally said.

"Who knows? Go get a job in another city, I suppose. Cobra doesn't know either. Oh, by the way, Milo, I don't know how many letters Penny's written you—"

"One."

"Yeah, well, don't you think it would be polite to drop her a note? Or, if you don't want to write, you could call her and just say hello."

"What for?"

"Well, she was nice enough to write to you. You don't want to hurt her feelings, do you?"

"Why not?"

"Look, let's just try not to be mean to people, okay? Let's not judge people and be critical of them. Let's try to accept everyone as they are."

"I'll tell that to Jastin Spitters."

"All right, point taken. I'll try to be more accepting of Jastin. There's just something about him. Something in my gut tells me not to trust that boy."

I thought once again about writing back to Penny. She was probably as shocked about Ms. Swinford as I was. We could bounce it off each other. We could also *commiserate*, *sympathize*, and *pity*. I knew what a rotten thing it was to not get a letter from somebody. Still, I couldn't bring myself to actually write Penny a letter. I wasn't sure I could bring myself to be nice to her. There are just some people who you're not sure you want to be nice to. Penny was like that for me.

# 7

## vacation–interrupt–discontinue–suspend–delay–wait

Sixth grade ended and summer vacation started. Mom was going to have to be gone all day, so she signed me up for every day camp and Scouting trip she could find. She wanted to make sure my summer was "well supervised."

Even so, Jastin and I usually got together in the evening for a couple hours of riding the bike trails, sometimes riding until dark. We had really built up the jumps, made the lips just right, fortified some of them with scraps of junk that we covered with dirt and smoothed down. We knew every twist and jump along those trails—every hillock and fork, every boulder, root, and rut. We knew where you had to duck the branches. We knew the muddy spots that never dried up. We knew the garbage piles and the rusted appliances, the abandoned car, the bike with no wheels, the bed frame, the coyote skeleton.

Midway through the summer, my dad showed up.

He had shaved off his beard. I'd never known him without his carefully groomed beard; his cheeks looked sunken and seedy. But his teeth looked great. He had gotten his braces off. He showed Mom and me his straightened, whitened smile.

Mom and Dad didn't act like enemies, but Mom had this slow burn going on. When she asked him why he'd been "such a stranger" to his son, Dad came up with a pretty good answer, actually. He said he'd had to focus an extraordinary amount of energy on "not being a stranger to himself." That answer didn't sit too well with Mom.

Dad and I went off to spend the day together.

I took him on a tour of the apartment complex and the trails where I rode my bike. I could tell he was pretty revolted by where we were living. "There's a lot of disturbed energy around here," he said. It didn't help that some lowlife had dumped a fresh load of garbage onto the trail the night before.

We went for a drive in Dad's rental car. It was a convertible, my first time ever riding in one. It was fun but a little hard to carry on a conversation. We ended up at a seafood place on Hood Canal. We sat outside at a picnic table and ate fish and chips and clam chowder.

"You used to be a vegetarian, didn't you?" I asked.

"Did I?"

"I thought that's why we never used the barbecue," I said.

"Interesting," Dad said. He seemed to give this a lot of thought. "Funny how these things evolve. Nowadays I'll eat pretty much anything except red meat."

I told him about my five jobs.

"Yes, that sounds like your mother," he said. "She's always been very task-oriented. Well, you want to hear what my five jobs are? Expand, experiment, piss people off, and break as many rules as you can get away with. How's that?"

"Pretty good," I said. "But that's only four."

"There you go," Dad said.

After a pause I said, "Did you know Ms. Swinford got fired?"

"Who? Your old teacher? Really?"

"I guess she pissed people off," I said.

"She was a hot little number," Dad said.

"Can a teacher get a job teaching somewhere else if she's been fired?" I asked.

"It depends on what she was fired for. They'll nail you for just about anything these days. Sex, drugs, they're always on the lookout for some violation." Dad was stroking his chin as if his fingers had forgotten he didn't have a beard anymore. "People tend to get so hung up about sex. Especially if it's a teacher doing it with a student. I mean, come on, if you're discreet about it, it can be a fairly enjoyable and salubrious thing for all parties involved. It certainly was for me and Gina. I told you about Gina, didn't I?"

"The one who was wise beyond her years, who you had the dalliance with?"

"We both grew immensely from it."

Dad filled me in on what he'd been doing the past year. He'd spent the first half of the year living in northern California with Gina. Then he and Gina had split up and he found himself in Montana with a new lady friend named Rita. Gina and the baby moved to Oregon.

"Baby?" I said.

"Oh yes, just for the record, in case you're interested in these family-tree things, little Grace is your half sister."

"I have a half sister?"

"She's only four months old," Dad said. "Cute, very cute, but not a bit functional. And such big hands! Gigantic hands!"

"I'm not an only child anymore," I said in wonder.

"I've been doing a lot of soul work," Dad said. "And I got a vasectomy. I'll be damned if I'll have any more kids."

"You don't smoke your pipe anymore."

"No, I gave that up. Gave up the mind-altering substances, too. I've been making some exciting discoveries about myself, Milo. I think I'm on to an exciting new philosophy."

"Do you think I'm ready to understand it?"

Dad looked at me. "You tell me. Do you feel a burning desire to know the truth?"

I considered this. Mostly I thought about riding my bike on the trails. The newest jump Jastin and I had rigged up. I thought about how I wished I could spend the whole summer wild and free, riding my bike and playing baseball and swimming in the cabana pool. Instead of having to go to supervised day camps, which were just glorified babysitters.

I felt ashamed.

When I didn't answer right away, Dad said, "Don't worry, you're getting there, you're maturing. Just the fact that you asked about it at all is a sign that you're coming of age. That hunger is waking up in you. We'll have to work on getting you to come visit Rita and me in Montana. You'll feel an amazing sense of liberation on the prairie."

"I'd like that," I said. "I'd like to feel liberated."

"It's good to hear you say that," Dad said. "Believe me, on the prairie, you'll be even more receptive to the higher concepts of my philosophy. It's exciting to see you embarking on the passage into manhood."

# Seventh Grade

§

hoping–desiring–yearning–nostalgia–craving–
aspiration–fantasy–wishful thinking–unreality

The rest of the summer I was hoping to hear from Dad about visiting Montana. Finally he telephoned in September. He sounded in very good spirits, even though he and Rita had split up. He'd also split Montana. Montana, he said, was stressful. I figured there must have been a lot of low-flying insects in Montana.

As seventh grade cranked up, I concentrated on my big five jobs. I played on the school football team and went to all the Scout meetings. I managed to stay out of trouble, even though there seemed to be a lot of it around me, especially at the Bon Repos. One day after school in the early fall, I was at my bedroom desk doing homework when I heard three gunshots. *Pop. Pop-pop.*

I got up and looked out my window, keeping my head down just in case there were bullets flying. It was a good thing Mom wasn't home; this probably would have upset her. Lately she'd been a roller coaster of emotions. One minute she'd be bitching at me about something, the next writing a letter to a politician, or flatlined on the couch with a damp cloth on her forehead, or pacing around the apartment like a wild-haired harpy, or chomping on her nails while studying one of her textbooks. Or talking on the phone to Aunt Shan or Grandma Nordquist.

"If I can just get him through middle school," she'd say into the phone.

Sometimes it seemed to me like it was going to be more of a challenge getting *her* through middle school.

All I needed was a Trail Tiger 300 TZ motorbike. Every chance I got, I showed her the ad in a magazine. "This is it. This is all I want. This can be Christmas *and* birthday. This will take me right into manhood. You'll never have to worry about me if you get me this. This will keep me out of trouble and *get me through middle school*."

"Sorry. No."

"Why not?"

"We can't afford it. It's too dangerous."

"Not if you use a helmet."

"And where would we keep it? And it would break or get stolen or you'd outgrow it or get tired of it."

"But I—"

"And I don't even know if it's legal for a thirteen-year-old to ride a motorbike in the woods. Oh, and did I mention we can't afford it?"

"It'll help me outrun the drug dealers."

She smiled. "Drug dealers." Then she looked at me again and frowned. "You're kidding, right?"

So it was a good thing Mom wasn't around as I peered out my window looking for the source of those gunshots. Now I heard sirens. Police cars drove up on the lawn between buildings. A SWAT team busily assembled itself. They looked like a bunch of college guys getting ready to pull a fraternity stunt.

Then I spotted him. A skinny man in a too-small T-shirt was standing on the balcony of Building F waving a gun around in his right hand and alternately yelling at the SWAT team below and at somebody inside the apartment.

As I watched the show from my window, I heard scrabbling sounds overhead; it had to be SWAT guys on my roof directly above me. At any second I expected to see the gunman get picked off by a sniper shot. There was a part of me that hoped the man would make a daring escape. But another part of me wanted to see what it would look like, the sight of a man dying, his face contorting in the moment of death, whether I'd see his soul float out of him.

I felt sorry for the man. His face was so full of anguish. Something had broken him. What? How?

How could life break you like that? I wanted to know.

Maybe I even had a burning desire to know.

How come life was so mean?

For some reason, I thought of Ms. Swinford. I could almost hear her voice as she talked about Switzerland, the Alpine meadows, beautiful lofty meadows, fresh air, "I wave my hat to all I meet!" That was life, too, wasn't it? How could *that* be life, and this man on the balcony also be life? What was the truth?

Four uniformed officers appeared on the roof of Building F. In about three seconds they moved across the roof and jumped onto the balcony where the man was standing. They were on top of him before he could lift his gun above the railing. They buried him. When they stood him back up, he was wearing handcuffs and crying and flailing around as though trying to escape from the handcuffs. They dragged him into the apartment, out of sight. A minute later they came out on ground level and hauled him over to a police car and put him into the backseat, and the police car drove away.

It was starting to get dark out. The lights along the walkways came on. I wondered where Mom was. She was late.

When she finally got home, there were still a couple of cop cars hanging around.

"Sorry I'm late," she said. She put the kettle on for tea and bustled around the kitchen. "I had the worst day. We had to do a lab assignment and I got my inlays and overlays all mixed up. Then I missed my bus. How was your day? Anything new and exciting going on? What are those police cars doing out there?"

"A distraught man over in Building F was shooting a gun

on the balcony," I said. "A SWAT team came and took him out. They jumped down on him from the roof. He's okay. They took him away in handcuffs."

She turned and looked at me with the trace of a smile on her face. The kettle started boiling.

It took me a while to convince her I wasn't kidding, but finally I succeeded.

"What next?" she yelled. She paced around the apartment, rubbing her elbows and saying "God, God, God" and raking her fingers through her hair. "I've got to get you out of this place! How did we end up living here? Whose idea was it? How did I let them talk me into this? This is no place for my child to grow up!"

I tried to remember what my dad had told me that one time, something about how we're the protagonist of our own stories, and how we blame others for how messed up we are and see ourselves as victims. I hadn't really understood it at the time, but now it made more sense to me.

"Why don't you sit down," I finally said to my mom.

I hadn't tried to sound commanding or forceful or anything. I just said it gently, but the sound of my own voice startled me. It sounded deeper than usual.

Mom must have noticed it, too. She sat.

"There's nothing to get all whacked out about," I said. Unfortunately, my voice had gone back to being a normal kid voice.

My mom started biting her nails. She had puffy purple rings under her eyes.

"We'll be okay," I said again.

"You probably don't mind living here at all," she said, looking off somewhere. "If it were up to you, you'd probably want to stay here. You can run wild here. We should have moved to North Pilchuck. Your grandmother offered to let us stay with her. I could have gotten a job as a waitress or something—anything—all I had to do was say I'm Rom Nordquist's daughter. But no, I didn't do that. Oh no, I needed to get trained for a *career*, a *real* career with a *future*, so we can afford to live in Seattle again someday. What was I thinking? How could I have been so *stupid*? It was that stupid life coach, he's the one, he talked me into this. Him and Shan. They kept saying, 'There's no real future in a small town like North Pilchuck. There's nothing there anymore.' Well, maybe not, but at least it doesn't have SWAT teams roaming around and madmen shooting guns off balconies! At least they know your name in North Pilchuck! Even the milkman knows your name!"

She was getting herself worked up again. I said, "Okay, let's move to North Pilchuck so we can have a milkman who knows our name."

That made her relax a bit, and she smiled.

Then I said, "You didn't make a mistake. You did the right thing. It'll be all right. You'll see."

I thought of that guy on the balcony, that look on his face. I was talking to him, too.

# 9

## get–receive–experience–suffer–ache–irritate–enrage–incite–propel–launch

Christmas came, and I didn't get the Trail Tiger 300 TZ motorbike. I figured I still had a shot at it for my thirteenth birthday in April, so I kept the magazine ad in plain sight so Mom would see it. But it didn't look promising.

The month before my birthday, I got another postcard from Dad. This one was from Bali. Where in the heck was Bali? Indonesia? Micronesia? He said he was working with two incredibly awakened Masters of Transformational Technique. This time he included his return address in Bali, a PO box. So I wrote him a letter.

Dear Dad,

I have made some good progress since the last time I talked to you as far as having a burning desire for truth, but

59

unfortunately I am stuck on just one thing. I can't think about anything but this new motorbike. I have included the ad for the motorbike so you can see what I am talking about. I told Mom that this is all I wanted for my birthday and Christmas but she says we don't have the money. I was wondering, since my birthday is coming up (April 5), if there is any way you could possibly send the money to me or ask the Masters of Transformational Technique to help manifest it. Like I said, I will include the ad for the motorbike so you know which one I am talking about.

Milo

I folded up the ad and put it in the envelope with the letter and mailed it off.

A few days before my birthday I got another postcard from Dad. He said I had misunderstood what the Masters of Transformational Technique were all about. He said we all need to detach ourselves from *outcome*. "Trust in the process," he wrote. "The Universe will work out the details. Travel light, dude."

• • •

"I'm sorry you're mad you didn't get a motorbike," my mom said on my birthday. "I just couldn't buy you something like that. You knew it all along."

"No, I didn't."

"Yes, you did."

"No, I didn't. Why couldn't you just get me something I

wanted for a change? You and Dad split up, you wrestled me out of my happy home and dragged me to these broken-down apartments, and all I wanted was a motorbike."

"I think you mean wrested, not wrestled."

"It was such a simple request," I said. "I would have gotten a paper route to pay for the gas and upkeep. But why should I get a paper route now? Why should I do anything? I'm a bitter victim. I've been victimized. It's the story of my life."

"I'm sorry to hear you're bitter."

"That only escalates my bitterness."

Over the next few weeks I slacked off in school, let my homework slide, and broke as many rules as I could get away with. The hell with being good. One afternoon I busted a bunch of bottles on the playground. One by one I flung each bottle up into the air above my head and watched it plummet down to the pavement and shatter. The noise of breaking bottles sounded evil and thrilling.

Somebody reported me.

The counselor called me into his office. He wanted to know what was going on.

I was tempted to tell him the truth: I was pissed off that I had not gotten a motorbike for my birthday. It was unfair. Here I was doing everything I was supposed to do, being strong for my mother, playing by the rules. And what did I get out of it? What was the point of being good when you didn't even get rewarded for it?

I could have added that I missed my father. That would

have ramped up the drama. And my fifth-grade teacher, how I missed her beautiful images and songs of Switzerland.

I didn't say any of that to the counselor, though, because it would have sounded stupid and whiny. However, I was not beyond trying to scrape up a little sympathy, so I told him that April was a tough month for me.

"Why is that?"

"Oh . . . well . . . it's my birthday. And it's the month my dad walked out of my life after he pushed my mother through the coffee table."

The counselor's face lit up. He opened his notebook and started writing.

• • •

Unfortunately, the counselor called my mom.

*"I am not going to have you pulling this crap!"*

She yelled so loud, babies started crying and dogs started barking in nearby apartments.

"I'll send you to military school, so help me God, if you start acting like a hoodlum!"

"You can't afford military school."

"I'll get you in on a scholarship! I'll take out a loan! You just try me!"

I didn't bother saying anything. Somehow, my mind had made a leap. The truth had always been there staring at me, and now I saw it: I didn't have to do what she told me.

I didn't have to do what anyone told me. I didn't have to fight about it or explain. I only had to create a space around myself and know that I was in control.

I would have to share this realization with my dad. He would probably understand it. He would approve.

# 10

summer–growing season–heyday–prime–
mature–fit–strong–muscle

It was a sultry summer evening. My seventh-grade year had ended a week ago. Mom and I were sitting out on the balcony watching the sky change colors. Mom was taking a break from studying.

It had been a typical full summer day for me. Get up early and ride the trails with Jastin until it was time to go to day camp. Hang out there until three in the afternoon. Then come home to the empty apartment, gobble down some food, meet up with Jastin (he was almost always around), and ride the bike trails for another couple of hours. Finish off the evening with a jump into the cabana pool to wash the dust off.

There wasn't much time to go around breaking bottles

and finding out how much I was in control. It was just as well—better not to have Mom on my back.

Out on the balcony, Mom had her bare feet propped on a chair. She was wearing shorts and a Hawaiian-style bathing suit top, and drinking wine cooler from a chilled glass. Her brown hair had a pretty reddish tint to it.

A few minutes earlier, a couple of muscular twenty-something guys in no shirts and floral below-the-knee swim trunks had walked by and whistled at Mom on the balcony and flirted with her. But Mom didn't take any lip from them and they went on their way.

"Next week I start the apprenticeship at the lab," Mom said. "They ease us out of the classroom. I'll start getting paid an apprentice's wage in the fall. I'll still have to work at the bath store—but we're making headway, Milo, we are making headway. Maybe we ought to think about going to church every once in a while."

I didn't say anything. She was just talking.

"But Sunday morning is my only time to relax and lounge around and read the paper," she said. "Do you mind that we've never gone to church?"

"No."

"You don't feel a desire to learn about God and religion and that sort of thing?"

"No."

Bugs swirled around in the streetlights. A cool evening breeze came from somewhere in the direction of Canada. People were out on their balconies, talking, laughing, shouting in different languages.

"I don't know how your father does it."

"Does what?"

"Just goes his own way. Without any kind of plan. But I always have to have a plan. Maybe I ought to . . . God, Milo, I'm still young. I'm only thirty-seven, that's not that old. Maybe I ought to go out and find myself a rich man."

She didn't say anything for a while. We just sat quietly.

"Pretend I didn't say that, okay?" she said.

"Will do."

"I don't see any point to it sometimes, though, I really don't. Why do we make life so hard? It's not hard for your father. *He* doesn't struggle. What do you want, Milo? You're young, you've got the whole world if you want it, you've got all the hope. Don't say you want a motorbike. Say you want the moon and stars. Say you want to find the cure for cancer. But don't . . . don't leave me out of it. You know what really hurts? You're growing up and I'm missing out on it. I'm missing out on having a relationship with my son . . ."

She was getting herself all worked up again. Getting emotional.

"In a few years you'll be gone, and then where will I be? Working in some lab making false teeth. Don't grow up too fast, will you, Milo?"

• • •

That summer I got another letter from Penny.

This time it was five pages. I just skimmed it. It was all the same old Penny. She bragged about how she had won the Rising Star award at acting camp, bragged about her volleyball achievements, bragged about her jazz dancing. She said she was transferring to a new school for eighth grade—some hippie co-op or something. And maybe, she said, just maybe some Saturday night I'd be interested in coming to Teen Fellowship. That would be such fun.

Oh yes, such fun. Teen Fellowship. Car washes and sing-alongs. Why couldn't she have written me some memories about fifth grade? Why couldn't she have given me some news about Ms. Swinford? I wouldn't have skimmed that.

"P.S. Please write back!!! Love, Penny!!!"

• • •

The August before eighth grade started—a hot, sweltering August with blackberries ripening along the trails—I was invited to attend the Don Frisk Football Camp, conducted by several prominent high school coaches, not the least of whom was Don Frisk himself.

It was quite an honor to be invited. I was one of five "most promising eighth graders" who had been chosen by the Kangley Little League Football Association to attend this camp. Mom was so proud.

The reason I'd been invited to such a select football camp was that I was quick and I could tackle better than anyone. I was getting taller and putting on weight, and as a defensive lineman I could knife through the cracks in the offensive line and sack the quarterback. I had become phenomenal at blocking punts and placekicks. This coming season the head coach of the Kangley Middle School football team was planning to use me as a deadly weapon on passing downs, when the quarterback had to be pressured.

The coaches at the football camp called everybody "son." They'd all heard of my Grandpa Rom. "You're a heck of a tackler, son. Old Rom teach you how to tackle like that?"

"No, his daughter did," I said.

They put me on a weight-lifting program to bulk up for eighth grade.

# Eighth Grade

# 11

## skin–flesh–sensuality–carnality–lust–grab–pillage–destroy–annihilate–lay to waste

September was hot and dry, and the eighth-grade girls showed off a lot of skin—shorts, miniskirts, bare legs, bare shoulders, belly buttons. They wore makeup, too. I started feeling twinges of loneliness.

My mom would sometimes remind me that I didn't have any new friends and never invited anybody to come over.

I would remind *her* that I was so busy with school, football, basketball, baseball, and Scouts that I didn't have time for "friends." Besides, Jastin Spitters was my friend, even though we didn't talk very much. Anyway, talking was hugely overrated.

In eighth-grade English they made us write essays about things that we thought were important to us. I wrote an essay about the man waving the gun around on the balcony. I also wrote one about how people dumped their garbage in the woods at the Bon Repos. My teacher singled that one out and read it to the class, and for a day I felt special, the same way I used to feel just about every day in Ms. Swinford's class, singled out and chosen.

I tried to write an essay about what it means to have a burning desire for truth, but I had a hard time on that one because, unlike a gun or garbage, truth isn't something you can see or smell. I really needed some guidance on this from my dad, but he was about as invisible as truth was.

Sometimes I couldn't quite believe I was actually in eighth grade, my last year of middle school. I'd look at myself in the mirror and be totally shocked by the face of some stranger who wasn't me—and yet was kind of a friend, too.

I actually did try to be friendly toward people at school. I even *made an effort*. But I didn't see the point in talking just for the sake of filling up the silence. What I liked about Jastin was that we didn't have to talk. We could spend a whole Sunday together and not exchange a single word, and the day would fly by and we'd wish it would never end. Jastin was always free on Sundays because there was no mail to steal that day.

When I did talk, my voice sounded funny; it kept sliding down into deepness, and it finally stayed there. Mom bought me my own stick of deodorant.

• • •

In football we won our first three games by scores of 20–0, 28–7, and 13–6. Our defense was rock solid. I was a starting defensive lineman. Games were every Saturday at one o'clock, with practices every weeknight.

Mom couldn't make it to the Saturday games because of her job at the bath store, and she had to do a lot of arranging for me to get rides to and from practices and games. But plenty of the coaches and fathers had the hots for her and were happy to swing by the apartment and knock on the door to pick me up and maybe get a chance to say a quick howdy to Mom, if she happened to be home. I wondered if any of them were asking her out on dates. Every chance she got, she'd sit me down and pump me for details on the game she'd missed. She'd get this faraway look on her face and say, "Oh! I wish I could have seen that!"

When football season finally ended—we finished with a 6–2 record—Mom went with me to the end-of-season banquet. At the banquet, several people—parents, coaches, and teammates—asked me in front of my mom if I was going to play football next year for Kangley High School. I told them I didn't know where we were going to be next year.

After that she didn't bug me as much about making new friends.

By the time basketball season was in full swing, I was seeing less and less of Jastin Spitters. The bike trails were too muddy, and he was busier than ever, stealing mail and throwing his money around on girls. He offered to hook me up with some girls he knew.

I was tempted to give it a try. I didn't think hooking up with one of Jastin's girlfriends would violate any of my big five jobs. But I turned him down anyway. Not because I was afraid of breaking any rules, but because the girls Jastin knew were a whole lot more mature than I was, even though I did have my own stick of deodorant and hair on my legs.

There was still a big chasm between me and adulthood.

I was like that hiker kid in the "Happy Wanderer" song; I could "wave my hat to all I meet"—but that was as far as it went.

• • •

Basketball season ended, and baseball started up.

One Friday morning in March, I rode my bike to school as usual. After school, I hung out in the library and did my homework so that I could leave my books in my locker over the weekend. Then I went to the locker room and suited up for baseball practice and listened to all the locker-room chatter, and we all walked out to the field for baseball practice. All of this was routine. I finished up with practice around seven o'clock and rode my bike back to the Bon Repos just as it was getting dark.

As I got nearer to the apartments, I felt like something wasn't right. I rode up to our building, locked my bike as usual, and looked around. What was bugging me? I sniffed at the air and thought I smelled . . . mud.

I went upstairs to the apartment. Mom wasn't home yet. Fridays she had to work late at the lab. Nothing unusual about that. I made some Tuna Helper for dinner and ate half of it, leaving the other half for Mom, who was usually starving when she got home. I kept looking out the window at the dusk settling in. I stepped onto the balcony and raised my face to inhale the woods. Again, that mud smell.

Then I saw it.

A small road had been bulldozed into the woods. The bulldozer was parked in a clearing. Next to it I could just make out part of a dump truck and an excavator.

Early the following Monday morning, Mom and I watched from our living room window as they bulldozed the woods into oblivion.

"How lovely," Mom said. "They're going to put up more lovely apartments, just like these."

By Friday the woods were gone. Nonexistent. Nothing but acres of dirt, toppled stumps, and heavy equipment. Barren dirtscape.

# 12

exam–test–ordeal–endurance–surrender–
withdraw–pull out

In June Mom spent a solid week studying for her certificate exam. Aunt Shan came over and took me out to dinner while Mom studied. As we left the apartment and walked out to the parking lot, Shan stopped in her tracks and said, "My God. Didn't there used to be trees over there?"

Mom took the exam on a Saturday. I had a baseball game that day, and I couldn't keep my head in the game. I was too worried about how she'd do. I kept picturing her agonizing over the test questions. I just hoped she'd get through it without something terrible happening to her. She had so much riding on that exam; if she didn't pass, it might break her.

Then we had to wait for the results. The mail arrived each day as usual, and Mom pounced on it. Finally one afternoon it came — the Envelope. I was in the kitchen making a ham-and-lettuce sandwich and searching the fridge for the mayo. Mom put on her reading glasses and tore it open.

I watched her eyes scan the letter. I held the refrigerator door open. Mom looked up at me. There was one long frozen moment of blankness. I closed the refrigerator door. Then she started crying. I didn't know what to do, but somehow I knew enough to go over to her and put my arms around her and let her cry onto my shoulder for a while. While she was doing that, I managed to get a peek at the letter in her hand. She'd passed.

• • •

She was now a certified dental technician. She spent the next couple of weeks looking at all her job choices, and finally she accepted a job offer from a lab in Seattle that made false teeth, crowns, and bridges. Aunt Shan helped her find a rental in Seattle. We'd be moving out of the Bon Repos by the end of August. Moving back to Seattle.

To celebrate, Mom and I went into the mountains for a three-day hike. Each day we hiked to a new lake and camped next to it. We hardly saw any other human beings. Mom and I talked some but we were mostly quiet. I hadn't seen her so peaceful since before Dad left.

Being out in nature made me feel kind of peaceful, too. The silence was so deep and still, like the sky-blue lakes we camped beside. I found myself just standing and listening to that silence. It was always there. Even when you could hear other noises—birds, woodpeckers, wind in the trees—the silence was there, too. I felt like I was absorbing it. Our last night of camping, the sky was clear and full of stars, and after my mom had gone to sleep I sat on a log and looked up at them. I thought of the woods that had been next to our apartment. They hadn't been much, those scraggly woods littered with trash, but they'd been there for me every day for the past three years, and I had made them part of me, just like I'd made so many other things part of me—my bike, our old barbecue, my synonym book, Switzerland.

The stars were so incredibly still, but everything in my life was moving—either coming or going. Coming into my life, staying awhile, and then leaving. There was no standing still.

I wondered what was going to come along next.

• • •

The day before we moved out of the Bon Repos, I rode around on my bike looking for Jastin. I found him riding his bike along the side of the road by himself, holding his handlebars with one hand and drinking a soda with the other.

"Hey," I said, riding up alongside him.

"Hey. What's up?"

"I'm moving."

"*Moving?* When?"

"Tomorrow."

He slowed down on the gravel shoulder and came to a stop. I stopped just behind him. Cars were passing us on our left.

"Yeah, well, take it easy," he said.

"You, too."

"Good luck."

"Yeah," I said. "Good luck!"

He started pedaling down the gravel shoulder toward the mall. His tires raised up dust, and his shadow stretched out behind him. I kept my eyes on him as he got smaller and smaller, until he finally disappeared.

# Ninth Grade

# 13

start–begin–create–formulate–evolve–
blossom–flower–edelweiss

Mom and I started our new life in a new neighborhood in Seattle, about eight miles from our old neighborhood.

We rented the downstairs half of a seventy-five-year-old house on a street that was shaded by hundred-year-old trees. The owner of the house, Ditta, lived alone in the upstairs half and had two tabby cats. Ditta was ten years older than my mom and the two of them became instant friends, as if they'd always known each other. Mom was good at that.

At night I'd sit outside on the steps and pet Ditta's cats and look up at the sky. I listened to the traffic sounds and airplanes and the silence behind the sounds. I listened to the wind chimes on Ditta's front porch, and the harder I listened, the more I heard a pattern. The wind chimes were making a song, repeating a pattern of sound over and over. It gave me a weird feeling to think that there was music going on all the time. I wondered if these thoughts and feelings were like Dad's when he used to stand out at the barbecue gazing at things. He hadn't just been gazing, he'd been listening!

Another night, I walked down to the park, and I listened to some frogs croaking. I sat on a bench in the dark, and the croaking got louder and louder. And then I started to hear a pattern in the croaking, the same sounds repeating over and over. Even nature had it!

Something was happening in me, but I had no idea what it was. I thought maybe if I listened hard enough, I'd be able to figure out some truth. I wished I could talk to my dad about it. I wondered where he was, if he was safe, if he would have an explanation for what was happening in me. If he was forming a new philosophy. If he'd found a home. Mom and I had found one.

*Wishing you the best of luck in your new home . . .*

• • •

Seattle had a lot of high schools, and you were free to choose whichever one you wanted to go to. That is, if you registered on time. But since we'd moved at the last minute, I didn't have any choice in which high school I went to. Which meant I ended up being assigned to the least popular high school in Seattle. It was way down in the south end, in one of the poorest neighborhoods. The school had a bad reputation.

But hey, at least it wasn't Kangley. From my three years at the Bon Repos, I knew how to handle myself around tough guys. Football and weight lifting had given me some confidence, too. I didn't mind having to take the city bus downtown and then transfer to another bus to the south end.

I turned out for the freshman football team and I mostly played defense. It was a whole lot tougher in ninth grade than in middle school. I didn't stand out as a star, but I was reliable—I showed up to every practice and game and I did whatever jobs the coach wanted me to do. Like the year before, the coach usually shuffled me into the game in passing situations where I could rush the quarterback.

To my mom's disappointment, I quit Boy Scouts. It wasn't that I was tired of it or that I'd outgrown it or lost interest in it, exactly, but that I didn't care about earning badges or becoming an Eagle Scout or having "positive male role models." And besides, it would have been too much work to join a new troop and get used to a whole new bunch of Scouts.

So I'd chopped off a toe. Now I was down to four jobs.

Mom and I were in a nice groove. We were getting the chance to kick back and get reacquainted with each other. In the evening, we'd watch TV together. On Sunday mornings Mom would make pancakes and we'd read the Sunday newspaper and then clean the house. Sometimes she did yard work out in Ditta's backyard. I mowed the lawn. Mom talked a little about her job at the denture lab, but she also talked about her past and told me the story of how she and Dad had met in college, how brilliant and witty she'd thought he was.

One Sunday morning when Mom and I were sitting around reading the newspaper, my dad called from Mexico. I couldn't even remember the last time I had talked to him. He sounded a little disoriented.

"What are you doing in Mexico?" I asked him.

"Nothing much at the moment."

He explained that he'd been doing some work with a church in Guatemala for the past few months. He had met up with a Professor Stratton. Professor Lara Stratton. They'd built a hospital. He had learned Spanish. Professor Stratton had gone back to Pasadena, California. He was going to walk to Pasadena to see if he could track her down.

"It shouldn't be too difficult to track down a professor," he said.

"Did you say *walk*?" I said.

"Yes."

"You're going to walk from Mexico to Pasadena?"

"Yes."

"Why?"

"It seems like a good idea. I've been formulating a new

philosophy and it'll give me a chance to iron out a few wrinkles in my thinking."

"Won't it be dangerous?"

"Walking?" He laughed.

"I mean through Mexico."

"It'll be more dangerous walking through California," he said.

"Dad, take care of yourself," I said.

"I will, Milo. You take care of your mother. And yourself."

"Okay," I said. "I'd like to hear your philosophy. I think I'm more ready than I've ever been."

"I always knew the time would come," Dad said. "I never doubted that for a moment. Just keep going, Milo. Our paths are heading toward each other and they're going to intersect at the right time."

• • •

Penny's mom, Cobra, came over for coffee. She cornered me in the kitchen.

"Penny sends you a big hello. She's thinking she might give you a call one of these days, now that you're back in town."

Thanks for the warning, I thought. I asked if she'd heard anything new about Ms. Swinford.

"Valerie? Let me think . . . Do I know what happened to Valerie? I have no idea. I've never heard from her. I'm sure she's moved on to better things. I don't really think she was meant to be a public school teacher. I always sensed that she was . . . I don't know. Someplace else."

Someplace else.

Someplace like Switzerland.

That was it. She had gone back to Switzerland! Of course she had, why wouldn't she? That's what I would have done. She must have gone back to live with Uncle Cedric and Aunt Liesl. That made me feel good. Why hadn't it occurred to me before? My dad was walking across Mexico working on his new philosophy, and Ms. Swinford was on the Alpine slopes inhaling edelweiss. Things were looking up.

# 14
## happy–cheerful–radiant–bright–alert–vigilant–wary–suspicious–distrustful–faithless–unfaithful–betrayer

I was glad to see Mom happy, but after about two months she seemed a little too happy. Abnormally cheerful. She started wearing colorful sporty outfits on her walks around Green Lake with Ditta, and she wore perfume. I eyed her. I asked her what was going on.

Eventually she confessed.

"Okay, I met somebody. At my high school reunion."

"What high school reunion?"

"My twenty-year high school reunion. North Pilchuck High."

"You went to your reunion?"

"Yes, Milo. Three weeks ago, remember? I drove up to North Pilchuck and spent the entire weekend there? That was the reunion."

"So that's why you've been wearing perfume and getting dressed up."

Mom smiled. "Have I? I guess I have."

"So what is he, some guy who had a crush on you because you were the coach's daughter, only he was a total loser back then, but now he's not as much of a dud?"

"Not bad," Mom said. "Not *right*, but not bad. Where did that come from?"

"It's been done in about a hundred books and movies."

Mom smiled. "Okay. His name is Stephen Yamashita. We were in the same class. He was no dud. He was brainy *and* a hunk. He played football for my father. I'm the one who had the crush on him. We've sort of . . . Well, we've seen each other a few times since the reunion."

She started telling me what he'd been doing for the past twenty years since high school, but I stopped listening. My stomach was starting to feel queasy. Then I realized it wasn't my stomach. It was raw anger coming from somewhere in my legs and shooting up to my stomach. It was burning hot.

I remembered that summer night at the Bon Repos, we'd been sitting out on the balcony, and Mom had said, "Don't leave me out of it . . . Don't grow up too fast." I had made a point of remembering those words. I had thought, Okay, I'll do my jobs, I'll do what you want. Not only will I stay out of trouble and do sports and make it through middle school, but I won't grow up too damn fast. I won't try too hard to cross that chasm into maturity or whatever you want to call it. And what was my reward for sticking by my mom and doing my jobs when I could have been out being wild and experimenting with drugs and doing whatever I felt like doing? What was my reward for hanging around this new house in the evenings and watching TV and mowing the lawn and listening to her stories when I could be out there following my own free spirit?

She'd gotten herself a boyfriend. Some jackass slob. That was my reward.

I felt like a total chump.

• • •

"You don't want to talk about this?" she said a couple days later.

I didn't say anything.

"You refuse to talk about this, is that right?" she said.

I still said nothing.

I had been giving her the silent treatment for two days.

What was weird was that I was also sort of watching myself give her the silent treatment.

Part of me felt like going out and breaking bottles in the school yard again. And maybe experimenting with worse things. Just to be totally rebellious and see how much trouble I could get into. See how serious she was about that military school threat.

But the other part of me was fascinated with watching myself refuse to talk to Mom.

One night I was out on the steps petting Ditta's cats and thinking about how angry I felt. I thought about the word *angry*, and that made me remember the synonym game. Maybe my anger was trying to tell me something. I went and got my synonym book and looked up the words *anger* and *angry*. I thumbed back and forth in the book, following different trails, nouns, verbs, adjectives. *Bitter, slow burn, stormy, cranky, seething, rebellious. Rebellious* led to *traitor*, which led to *betrayal. Betrayed, double-crossed, deserted.* Yes, yes, yes, all of that was me. *Deserted, abandoned.* Yes, I was a victim of *disloyalty, treachery*.

*Hm, well, this game sucks . . .*

Remembering Ms. Swinford, I found myself grinning. It struck me as really weird that here I was feeling awful in my gut, but also looking up the very words I was feeling. The more I flipped back and forth to different synonyms, the more I realized that I might feel the words in my gut all right, but I couldn't really blame my mom for any of them. She hadn't really *created* any of those words that I was feeling. All she had done was meet a guy. She hadn't stabbed me in the back. Whatever awfulness I was feeling wasn't really her fault. She hadn't done anything to me.

Once again, I felt like I'd made a big discovery, but I needed to run it by my dad and see what he thought.

The next time I saw my mom, she said, "Look, Milo, let's just be level-headed about this for one moment and talk about it. Can't we at least do that?"

"Sure," I said.

That stopped her for a second. I had spoken. "We can?"

"Sure," I said.

"We're talking about Stephen, right?"

"You bet."

"Oh . . . well, good. That's . . . good news. I'm glad you're talking again. What I wanted to say is, it's way too early in the game to make this thing with Stephen into a great big problem. I mean, come on, can't we just kind of lay it out on the table? Can't I at least invite him over so you can meet him?"

"Okay," I said.

That really startled her.

Then she looked kind of pleased with herself, like she was thinking, *Ah, you see that, Cori? All you had to do was reason with him a little and you'd bring him around. Good job.*

He came over Saturday morning.

It was raining and his hair was all wet. He had dark, straight hair, going gray throughout, as if he'd sneezed in chalk dust.

His gray raincoat matched the gray in his hair.

"Here, Stephen, let me take your coat."

"Ah, thanks, Cori."

He smiled and rubbed his hands together eagerly. He was wearing a blue button-down dress shirt. It looked stiff and starched, and it bunched up where it was tucked inside his narrow belt. He mentioned how hard it was to find parking around here.

Mom introduced us and we shook hands. I gave him another quick glance. He had broad shoulders and a solid, powerful neck. I played it very cool.

She had probably warned him that her son might be a little *cool, cold, frosty, unfriendly, unwelcoming.*

"Great to finally meet you, Milo. Your mom is a big fan of yours. You can call me Stephen, of course. As opposed to, uh, you know, Mr. Yamashita."

He chuckled. He seemed kind of nervous. I felt like I had the upper hand. I said in a dry, smart-ass voice, "How about *Steve?*"

"Nah, Steve's not really my cup of tea," he said.

Mom was sweating. Good, I thought.

She sat Stephen down at her spotless kitchen table. She acted prim and attentive whenever he said something directly to her. She kept her chin up, her posture erect, her mouth frozen in a smile, her teeth together, her eyes busy and alert, like a beauty pageant contestant. She served him coffee and a hunk of the coffee cake that she had spent half the night laboring over and cussing at. She offered me a piece, but I just laughed and said "No, thank you!" in a particularly meaningful way, hoping that I'd make Stephen wonder if I knew some dirty inside secret about this coffee cake.

Stephen started talking with his mouth full of coffee cake about how challenging the parking situation was, not only in our neighborhood but in many other neighborhoods of Seattle. He seemed really obsessed with parking issues. Mom kept sliding looks at me as if she were afraid I was going to start doing things to scare her man away, like call him Steve or pee on the floor to mark my territory.

Stephen gripped his mug with both hands and made approving remarks about the coffee cake while washing it down with coffee. He turned down the offer of a second helping.

After he left, Mom let out a long breath and said, "Well, that went well, don't you think? Quite well."

No comment from me.

That night I heard Mom on the phone saying, "Oh, Shan, he loved the coffee cake. He just *raved* about it."

# 15

football–game–amusement–diversion–
recreation–romp–spree–frolic–giggle–clown

I was playing defensive end in the last football game of
the season. It was a home game, a dark muddy miserable
Wednesday afternoon in the first week of November. It
wasn't even four o'clock and they'd already turned the field
lights on. My body was on the field, but my mind was out
in space. I just wanted the season to be over. I was looking
forward to having the next two days off before basketball
practices started up the following Monday. Two whole af-
ternoons with nowhere I had to be after school. I had no
idea what I was going to do, but I wanted to do something
different, something out of the ordinary.

I happened to look over at the sideline, and I noticed
Stephen there. He was standing down at the fifteen-yard
line by himself, wearing his gray raincoat.

Seeing that I'd spotted him, he hoisted his chin and gave me a thumbs-up.

I shook my head. The guy must really have it bad for my mom. Bad enough that he'd come here all by himself and stand on the fifteen-yard line at the last lousy game of the season.

We lost the game 12–6.

The following day I turned in my football gear until next season and took off into the gray, bleak afternoon rain.

Where to go?

I could go anywhere on my bus pass. I could walk to any bus stop and hop on whatever random bus happened to pull up, paying no attention to what number it was or what direction it was going, just riding to whatever strange neighborhood it took me to.

That's exactly what I did. As the rain fell steadily, I chose the least crowded bus and flashed the driver my bus pass. Then all I had to do was sit back and enjoy the ride and look out at the rainy street and the snarled traffic. I watched the people get on and off. Some of them smelled bad and muttered to themselves, others didn't.

Finally, after about twenty stops and a half-hour ride, I saw a street that looked inviting, and I got off the bus. I pretended I was a traveler in a foreign city. I'd never been to this neighborhood before, and yet people lived here, they shopped here, this street was familiar to them, and I was a tourist. I walked down the street, looking at the shops. I figured out that the name of this neighborhood was Maple Leaf. I'd never heard of it, didn't know Seattle even had a neighborhood called Maple Leaf. I walked into an espresso place and ordered a hot chocolate and sat at a table by the window and watched the people walk by on the sidewalk. I felt happy, free, touristy, like a world traveler. I could even have been in Switzerland! This could be a Swiss village, and there was the Matterhorn, just behind those clouds. I sipped my hot chocolate. Then I went outside and hopped on a bus that happened to be passing by.

I made it home around dinnertime.

I did the same thing on Friday. Different buses, different neighborhoods. I felt worldly, not lonely at all, and I liked traveling solo, because I didn't have to think or plan, everything was spontaneous.

That weekend I thought about basketball practice on Monday. I thought about all the different neighborhoods in Seattle I could travel to. I could ride a different bus every day and hit every neighborhood. I could do some sightseeing. I could look at the buildings and the architecture, like my parents used to do together.

On Sunday I informed my mom that I had decided not to turn out for basketball. Then I prepared for the lecture.

"Oh, great. See? It's a downward spiral. First Boy Scouts, and now basketball. What are you going to do instead? There are other winter sports. Or how about—"

"I want some free time after school for a while," I said.

"To do what?"

"I've kind of got a new pastime."

"And that would be?"

"I'm going to ride buses around and explore Seattle."

"Ride buses."

"Yeah. I can go to different neighborhoods and libraries and parks and museums and just see the world. Just like a tourist."

"Milo, you're scaring me. You sound crazy. You sound like your father. Have you been talking to your father?"

"No."

"It just sounds like you're wasting time. It's not productive."

"Football took up all my time after school. I'd like to take a break."

"A break. You know what a break is? It's a recipe for trouble. I don't know about this bus riding thing, Milo."

"I don't want to have to be somewhere at a certain time."

"Yeah, you want to be a free spirit. That sounds even more like your father."

Mom searched my eyes. Probably checking if I was on drugs or something. I didn't know why I felt so calm. In the past I would have been all nervous that Mom was going to yell me into submission, totally cow me.

"Is it your high school? Do you want to try to transfer to one closer to home?"

"No, the school's fine."

Mom studied me some more.

"You need to find a friend. If you had a friend—"

"Yeah, yeah, I know."

"What's *really* going on here?" she said.

"What do you mean?"

"All right, let's get it out in the open. This is about Stephen, isn't it."

"What?"

"This is my punishment. You punished me when I didn't buy you a motorbike, and now you're punishing me for meeting Stephen."

At first I was going to tell her to shove it. But then I thought a more mature response would be to simply turn and make a dignified exit from the room. I had never done that before, and for some reason I had always wanted the opportunity to make a dignified exit from a room, preferably when the other person is right in the middle of ragging on you. One of these days I was going to make a dignified exit from somewhere. But not today, not that Sunday.

For a moment I didn't do anything but stand still. Finally I said, "From now on, whenever I do something, and you're kind of wondering why I did it, you can just assume *it doesn't have anything to do with Stephen*. Okay?"

Mom was speechless for a second. Then she said, "I guess."

That was all she said. Amazing. *She* was the one who was cowed.

I didn't know what had just happened, but I was impressed.

Stephen showed up at Grandma Nordquist's house in North Pilchuck for Thanksgiving.

Aunt Shan was there, too. Aunt Shan had never been married, and I saw her checking Stephen out. She asked him where his children were spending Thanksgiving. Didn't he have *three children* from a previous marriage?

Stephen explained that his three children, Tarquillin, Fawn, and Lyric, were spending Thanksgiving with their maternal grandparents. Tarquillin, the boy, was thirteen, and Fawn and Lyric were twelve and eleven.

"What delightful names," Shan said. "Tarquillin. Do you call him Tarq for short?"

"Oh no," Stephen said. "Beth called him 'Tarkie' once, and he, uh, didn't like it."

"It wasn't his cup of tea," I said.

Everyone looked at me.

Later, Stephen hauled Grandma Nordquist's ancient toolbox out to the shed to see if he could fix the throttle on her lawn mower in preparation for spring. While he was out there freezing his ass off, Grandma, Shan, and Mom sat in the living room talking about him, speculating on the origin of his children's names and admiring the three bouquets he had brought "for three lovely ladies."

How pathetic, I thought. How god-awful pathetic. To be a grownup. To spend part of your Thanksgiving in a freezing shed trying to fix the lousy lawn mower of an old lady you didn't even know, while your girlfriend and her big sister and mother discussed your flowers and What Happened to Your First Wife.

*Depressing* and *pathetic* didn't even seem like strong enough words. When I got home from Grandma's, I looked up synonyms of *pathetic*, but I found the antonyms to be much more appropriate: *farcical, ludicrous, ridiculous*.

· · ·

Over Christmas break, Stephen took his three children to Hawaii. When he got back, he gave Mom a stack of photos. Mom showed them to Shan in the kitchen.

Shan went through them one by one. I eavesdropped from the other room.

"What lovely kids. Well, the girls, at least—that lovely blend of Asian and Caucasian. The boy looks a bit odd. Tarquillin. Why doesn't he smile or look at the camera? My God, it certainly looks like they were staying at a *very* expensive resort. Oh, those girls are just dolls. Cori, does this man have money?"

"He's . . . comfortable," I heard Mom say.

"Now listen to me, little sister. You've got a fourteen-year-old son. You've moved him too many times to too many schools in the past four years. How much has his father given him? How much quality time have you spent with him? How many vacations have you taken with him? It's not too late. Stephen Yamashita is a good man and he seems to have money. Want my advice? Marry him, quit your job, stay home, and enjoy the time you have left with your son, because he's going to grow up so fast you won't know what hit you."

"Shan," I heard my mom say, "you are just way, way out of line. You're jumping the gun."

"Honey, jumping the gun's the surest way to win."

• • •

Mom and Stephen were getting so serious, they were going to counseling together. I guess they had to pay somebody to tell them what to do next.

Stephen was friendly toward me but he didn't overdo it, which I appreciated. He gave me plenty of space. I could tell he was trying to get on my good side.

If I had tried a little harder, I probably could have hated his guts. I could have at least tested him to see how hard he was willing to work for my mom. But I couldn't blame him for falling for my mom. The mere fact that two old people like my mom and Stephen could get together—it was kind of miraculous in a way.

My biggest complaint about Stephen was that he talked with his mouth full. He took Mom and me out to dinner at his favorite steak house.

"I happen to think," he said while chewing his steak, "that Rom Nordquist [chew chew] was quite possibly one of the top [chew chew, sip of wine, chew chew] ten high school football coaches in this state's history."

"Really?" Mom said. "That's quite a statement. You're

not just saying that because you're going out with his daughter, are you?"

"Nah-hah-hah," Stephen said. "Nor am I just saying it because I happened to play football for him for three years."

For some reason that whole evening just nauseated the crap out of me. The giggly yuk-yukking between him and my mom, the little nudges they gave each other. They were acting like horny teenagers. What bugged me most was that these people, these grownups, did not seem much further along than I was.

# 16

meet–assemble–participate–join–combine–mix–
scramble–confuse–screw up–perplex–mystify

I had yet to meet Stephen's three children. When I was around Stephen and he happened to mention them, I always got the feeling that he was straining to make them sound normal. Which probably meant they were monsters.

"They're not monsters," Mom said to me. "I've been over to Stephen's house and met them. They're wonderful kids. Really. I wouldn't lie. They miss Beth, of course."

"Beth?"

"Stephen's first wife."

"What happened to her?"

Mom looked at me. "What do you mean, what happened to her?"

"Did they get a divorce or what?"

"Milo, his wife died of leukemia. I know for a fact I've mentioned that to you at least twice. Don't you ever listen?"

"Huh." I shook my head. "Do the children live with him?"

"Yes. But they're very close to Beth's parents. Actually, Beth's parents live . . . on the same cul-de-sac."

When Mom said "on the same cul-de-sac," the words seemed to stick in her throat. The ghost of the dead wife bothered Mom. When she and Shan and Ditta talked about her, they had a special name for her—they always referred to her as "Megabeth."

• • •

"I do believe they're talking prenup," Aunt Shan told me one day when Mom wasn't there. "If they *are* talking prenup, then he's even richer than I thought he was."

"They're talking what?"

Shan peered at me. "Prenup. *Prenup.* Don't you know what a prenup is? Don't they teach you anything in that high school?"

"Prenuptial agreement?" I said.

"Thank you. You've redeemed my faith in the educational system."

"What exactly is it, though?"

"It's what rich people do to protect their riches in case they get a divorce."

"So if you sign a prenup, you're betting the marriage isn't going to last?"

"Bingo. Nothing's guaranteed to last, kiddo. You should know that well enough by now."

• • •

In February, Mom offered to buy me an early birthday present: a twenty-visit pass to the batting cages. "Now's the time to start getting in shape for baseball season, don't you think?" she said.

She seemed prepared when I told her I had decided I wasn't going to play baseball that spring. She closed her eyes for a couple of seconds and breathed.

"You're just going to keep on doing nothing, then."

"I'm going to take it one day at a time and see where the path takes me."

She rolled her eyes. "That's your father talking again."

"What's so bad about that?"

"I don't see the value. I don't see the productivity. What're you going to do after school, sit around and think big thoughts and be a philosopher? Ride the buses around town? Not join any clubs or participate in any school activities? Is that how you're going to show you're in control of your life?"

"No . . ."

"You dropped Scouts, you dropped basketball, you're dropping baseball. You roam around by yourself—at least, I assume it's by yourself. You're a lone wolf."

"What do you want me to do, join a gang?"

"Will you at least consider doing one small thing for me?"

"What's that?"

"Give Teen Fellowship a try."

"You mean the one Penny belongs to?"

"Yeah. I just want you to be involved in something. It's important at your age to have social contacts. You know, networking. And I want you to believe in something. I don't necessarily mean religion or God—although that wouldn't be a bad place to start. I mean . . . being part of something larger than yourself—a community. That's what I'm saying."

"I'll think about it."

"Will you?"

"Yeah, but I don't think Teen Fellowship is for me."

"How do you know if you don't give it a chance? Cobra says that Penny just loves it."

"Yeah, I'll bet Penny runs the whole thing. She always has to take over everything."

"How about if I tell Cobra to have Penny give you a call? You can talk to Penny about it. Air your concerns with her."

• • •

Penny called me that night around ten o'clock. I was in bed reading. Mom tapped on my bedroom door and brought the cordless phone in and handed it to me. I waited for her to leave me alone before I said hello.

"Hi, Milo, it's me, Penny. How are you? I'm not calling too late, am I? It's been a long time, hasn't it? Boy, your voice has gotten deeper."

She said a lot more. It was weird hearing this voice I hadn't heard since fifth grade. She sounded exactly the same. I pictured her face, the last time I'd seen it, at that potluck almost four years ago. I pictured the way she had looked sitting at her desk in Ms. Swinford's classroom.

She said her poem "I Give Notice" had won a young poets contest. She talked about Teen Fellowship. She said it was held in the basement of that old church around the corner from my old house. They ate pizza and had guest speakers and socialized and "I know it doesn't sound like all that much fun, but it really is, because the people are so cool, I mean that's what makes all the difference, it's just that the people are very real and honest, there's almost nobody who's a phony . . ."

Really? I thought. What about you? While she talked, I reached for my synonym book and looked up the word *phony* . . .

*fake, actor, poseur, gasbag, hypocrite, pretender* . . .
*Penny.*

I shut the book and put it aside.

When she finished talking, all I said was "Uh, thanks anyway, but I don't think I can make it. It doesn't sound like something I'd be into. That, uh, fellowship stuff."

It didn't come out sounding too nice. After we hung up, I turned off my light and tried to go to sleep, but I was worried I had hurt Penny's feelings. It started to dawn on me that I had not really hated Penny in fifth grade. I had just been pretending to hate her. It had been a game my friends and I had played. We had created a whole myth around Penny.

Well, I wasn't in fifth grade anymore. The game of pretend was long over. I wasn't the same person I'd been then. But what about Penny? She seemed exactly the same. It was very confusing. It had been four whole years since fifth grade. Yet it didn't seem that long ago at all. And that time seemed more real to me than any time since. Why was that? I just couldn't wrap my mind around it.

Maybe I would not be so confused if I just made more of an effort to be nice to Penny. Tried harder to be nice to people in general. Maybe it was that simple. Just try to be nicer.

In the morning, Mom asked me how the phone call had gone.

"Fine."

"Did she . . . ?"

"I told her no."

Mom's expression sagged. "Oh. You did."

"Yeah."

She shook her head. "You know, we are really going to have to work on your social life."

# 17

conversation–chatter–babble–gibberish–
nonsense–unintelligible–unknowable–
supernatural–transcendental–visionary–seer

In an effort to be more social and nicer to people, I tried making conversation with Stephen.

"What happened to your first wife?" I asked him. He and I were alone, sitting on the couch in the living room watching a college basketball game on TV. Mom was out in the kitchen.

"Didn't your mom tell you? Beth—my first wife—died of leukemia."

"That must have been rough."

"Yeah, it was. Rough on everybody. Yeah." He nodded.

We were silent. This silence started to get awkward. Why were some silences peaceful and some awkward? Fortunately, we had the basketball game to look at.

"It's tough losing somebody," Stephen said.

"I'll bet," I said.

"I mean I've . . . I think I've worked through most of it in therapy," he said. "I feel pretty sure I'm ready to move on. But the truth is, Milo, it was a long, excruciating death trudge."

Later, after Stephen had left, Mom said, "It seemed like you two were having a nice chat during the basketball game."

I didn't say anything.

She looked at me.

"It was a conversation, right?" she said.

"I don't remember."

"What do you think of him?"

"Who?"

"Stephen."

"Why doesn't he go by Steve?"

"Why don't you ask him?"

"I don't really care. And I don't think of him. You can add that to the list of things I don't do."

"Well, you were thoughtful enough to have a conversation with him, and I appreciate that, even though you're being kind of a butthead right now. But that's okay. You're okay with him. I realize you're not going to *admit* you're okay with him, but that's okay, too, because you'd tell me if you *weren't* okay with him, so I know you *are* okay with him."

"You must have learned all that crap from your therapist," I said.

"Therapists," Mom said. "Oh, listen, that reminds me—"

"Thera*pists?*" I stared at Mom. "How many do you have?"

"Two. They're a male-and-female partner team. They're helping Stephen and me put a plan together, and they think the time is right for you to meet Stephen's children. I was thinking dinner, here. I have to find out from Stephen what his kids will eat."

"Wait a minute, I'm still trying to get my mind around this. *Two* therapists. This is news to me."

"They're a team, Milo. I'm sure it isn't the first time you've heard about them."

"Do you have to pay double?"

Mom started to say something, but the phone rang.

At first she just glanced at it, as if she was going to let the voice mail take it. Then she hesitated (*What if it's Stephen?*) and picked it up.

Her face changed.

I could immediately tell it was my father.

Mom talked to him dully for a minute, then said, "Yes, he's right here." She handed me the phone.

I tried to think of the last time I had talked to my dad. I couldn't remember. There'd been several postcards, though. I'd saved them in my top drawer.

I put the phone up to my ear and heard his voice. "Milo? Hey, how's it going?"

"Dad? Pretty good. How's it going with you?"

"Good, very good. I'm building a kayak."

"Really? Wow."

"Lara and I are doing well— Er, we *were* doing well."

"You mean Professor Stratton?"

"Yes, yes. We split up, actually, but it was all for the best. It's all good, Milo."

"Where are you?"

"Arizona."

"In the desert?"

"Well, kind of."

"You're building a kayak in the desert?"

"There is water in Arizona, Milo."

"Is it hot down there—in the desert?"

"I try not to make critical judgments about climate. But there's an excellent vibration here, Milo, the most intense I've ever felt in my life. Why don't you come for a visit?"

"Me?"

"Yeah, how about it? I don't think it would kill you to take two or three days off from school. I'll pay for the plane ticket. Why don't you ask your mom."

"All right, hang on."

I put the phone against my stomach.

"Can I go to Arizona and visit Dad for a few days?"

"He invited you?"

"Yeah."

"Do you want to?"

"Yeah."

"You're sure? You don't mind missing some school?"

"Yeah, I'm sure. He's going to pay for the ticket."

Mom hesitated, then nodded.

"She says yes," I said to my dad.

"Fantastic."

"Ask him what he's doing for a living down there," Mom said.

I said into the phone, "Dad? She's curious to know what you're doing for a living down there."

"You don't really have to work in Arizona, Milo. The harmonic convergence is so intense here, there's an abundance of supply. It's like living by the ocean and dipping your hand into the ocean's abundance whenever you need water. There's simply no sense of scarcity here."

I put the phone against my stomach again. "He's not doing too much," I said.

Mom rolled her eyes. "Is he going to send a ticket, cash, what?"

"I'll send a money order," Dad said. "Have your mom book the flight to Phoenix. How's school going?"

"Good. It's going great. I've been riding around on the buses seeing a lot of the sights in Seattle. And I've been trying to listen closely to things."

"I'm really on to something here, Milo. I can't wait to share it with you. I may very well have found the secret. The key that unlocks the door to enlightenment. It's called the Cog."

"That sounds pretty cool," I said. I wondered if he was back into psychedelic drugs.

# 18

airport–runway–path–inquiry–exploration–
observation–detection–discovery–recognition–
cognize–the Cog

At the airport, my mom started crying. But it wasn't too embarrassing, because a lot of folks at the airport were crying. It was my first time at an airport, and I had never really seen with my own eyes so many people crying in one place, crying when they said goodbye and crying when they said hello. Actually, I kind of felt like crying, too.

But I went through security, and found my gate and a place to sit, and I waited. I had brought a few books along with me, but I was too busy sitting there trying to take it all in—the planes taxiing and taking off, the weary-looking travelers lolling around, people rushing everywhere, the mysterious announcements over the loudspeakers, the overhead TV monitors showing the news.

I felt like I was on an adventure—a journey. More awake and alive than I'd been for a long time.

When I got on the airplane, I sat down in my window seat and took out one of my books. I felt excited and scared and already a little homesick.

A business lady came walking down the aisle. She was carrying a briefcase in front of her. I thought she was going to sit in my row, and I noticed her face. Red lipstick, puffy apple-red cheeks, glasses, curly brown hair. My heart jumped. It was Ms. Swinford!

I must have been gaping at her like a lunatic, because as she came closer and noticed me, she glared back at me. I now realized it wasn't Ms. Swinford. I turned to the window, my face burning. Luckily, she didn't sit in my row, so I didn't have to explain to her why I'd been staring at her as if she were a ghost.

I had never really thought of Ms. Swinford as being any age. All teachers had seemed old to me, like parents. But now that I thought about it, she must have only been in her mid-twenties when she was my teacher. It had been her first year as a teacher, and she'd just graduated from college. She was twenty the year she'd lived in Switzerland, and that had only been a few years earlier.

The fact was, Ms. Swinford was only thirteen or fourteen years older than me. There was something exciting about that. It made her seem more human to me and less like a teacher, less like an actual grownup.

• • •

Dad picked me up at the Phoenix airport in a convertible that belonged to Tawny, his new lady friend. "I don't need a car of my own," he said. "I'm trying to keep my material possessions to a bare minimum." I hadn't seen him in two years. His reddish beard was once again full and bushy. His ponytail was still there, but his hair was thinner on top. He wore a khaki shirt with the top two buttons unbuttoned, showing his chest hair. He looked tanned and healthy, the way you'd expect somebody who lived in the desert and was building a kayak to look.

We drove for an hour out of Phoenix with the scenery flying by. The sun was glaringly bright and I had to get my sunglasses from my travel bag and put them on. The wind blasted back my hair.

The farther from Phoenix we drove, the more the traffic thinned out, and Dad turned onto some lesser highways and gunned it down the long straightaways. The air wasn't like the moist, humid Seattle air. This air was . . . well, it was the desert! Dry, thin air. Cacti standing in frozen mime poses along the highway. Craggy, jagged red bluffs. I had thought Arizona would be all flat and sandy, like the Sahara. But there were red rocks, cliffs, canyons, plateaus, mountains, trees. Quarries! Rushing rivers perfect for kayaking.

We drove into the small town where Dad lived. There were a lot of ex-hippies living up in the hills, artists, craftspeople, vegetarians. His house was adobe-style, with plenty of green leafy trees and shade. He showed me around the place and introduced me to some of the other people who lived in the house.

"Is this a commune?" I asked Dad, thinking of Penny's living situation.

"A commune? Well, no, I don't think I'd characterize it as a commune."

"Do these people all know about the Cogs, too?"

"What?"

"I mean, do you all—"

"First of all, it's *the Cog*, not the Cogs. We're all seekers on our own journey, Milo. Occasionally our paths intersect, but each one of our journeys is entirely our own. We're not a cult. The Cog speaks to each soul individually. Only a handful of people truly know the Cog."

"Are you one of that handful?" I asked.

"Yes, I am. The Cog found me."

"Can it find me?"

"Yes. Obviously."

"Why do you say 'obviously'?"

"Because you're here, aren't you? So it has found you."

"I don't know anything about that," I said. "I guess I need help learning about the Cog. But I'm ready to learn."

"Excellent."

"Would you mind being my guide or whatever?"

"Gladly, Milo."

"There's a lot I want to talk to you about."

"Good. We have three days. I'm here to listen. And teach."

When the sun went down, the whole western horizon blazed like red fire. We went in the house and made a fire of our own in a little sitting room. We had the room to ourselves; it was only a one-story rambler, but it was very spacious and had many wings and corridors, and no one else was around. The fire crackled from the dry sweet juniper wood. A set of windows looked out on the hulking shapes of the mountains.

"What is the Cog, anyway?" I asked Dad. "Why is it called the Cog?"

"It's from the Latin *cognoscere*. Which simply means 'to know.' As in *cog*-nize."

"What does it do? How do you use it?"

"You don't use it. It uses you."

"How does it use you?"

"By transforming you from the inside out. There's no way to explain that transformation in words. As soon as you try to explain the Cog, it vanishes. The Cog can only appear inside you, and then radiate out into actual life."

"How does it appear inside you?"

"Through your senses. The more fully you turn your senses to it, the clearer is the Cog."

"How do I turn my senses to it?"

"By choosing the right path."

"What is the right path?"

"Simple. It's the path of least resistance."

"How do I know which path that is?"

"When you notice yourself resisting, that's the wrong path. When you find yourself struggling and fighting, that's the path of more resistance, not of least resistance. It's quite obvious."

"So you don't do anything at all?"

"If you don't fight or resist, believe me, that will be all you'll need to do. The path of least resistance will open up. And that's where the Cog comes in. The Cog will only come once you've chosen the path of least resistance."

"How did all this come to you, Dad? How did you learn it? Did somebody show it to you? Did you read it in books?"

"A little of this, a little of that."

"Bali? Mexico?"

"The Masters of Transformational Technique in Bali had a very limited understanding of the Cog. As for Mexico, that was a total washout."

"Did you walk all the way to Pasadena?"

"No, no. Lara—Professor Stratton—came and picked me up in Tijuana. My God, that's a place I never want to see again. But while I was living in Pasadena with Lara, I went to a couple of lectures about the Cog, given by Ancient Highly Evolved Entities. Then when things were getting a bit strained between Lara and me, I enrolled in a nineteen-day Cog Immersion Retreat, which was happening in Taos. That's where I met Tawny, at the retreat. You'll get a chance to meet her. She lives in Sedona. That's about forty miles away."

I had so many more questions, I didn't know where to start.

"How's Cori doing, by the way?" Dad asked.

"Mom? Oh, she's great."

"She's met someone, hasn't she?"

"Yeah . . . How did you know?"

Dad tapped his head. "The Cog. I picked up on it when I spoke to her on the phone."

# 19

desert–wasteland–void–empty–blank–vacant–
available–handy–skillful–craftsman

Dad and I ate Mexican food and drove out into the desert and hiked the trails and rock cliffs. Dad loved rock climbing and he was very sure-footed. I thought he looked kind of nerdy in his black socks and shorts—the shorts were too long to be shorts and too short to be pants. I remembered all the times Mom had tried to get him to come out and play ball in the backyard. He'd never been coordinated at things like catching balls, and he'd get freaked out if some bee or dragonfly buzzed by him. But he had changed. He seemed to be very comfortable with the outdoors and nature and insects. He could climb rocks like a billy goat. I figured he must be on to some big truth; something had changed him, and I was going to try to learn from him any way I could.

He took me into the barn where he was building the kayak. All afternoon and evening we worked on it together. Time totally disappeared. He showed me what to do. We took these long narrow strips of wood—I think they were cedar and black walnut—and put them into a steamer so that we could bend them. The steam leaking out made me sweat.

Then we glued and stapled the strips onto the skeleton form. Dad showed me how to sand the strips with rough sandpaper. Always go with the grain, he told me, never against it. That's true with wood and it's true with life.

The smells of the leaking steam, fresh wood, and glue were delicious. I was very happy. It dawned on me that, wow, my dad and I were actually making something! I could hardly remember a time when we'd actually done a project together.

"Man, Dad, I didn't know you knew anything about building a kayak," I said.

He tapped his head again. "The Cog: I Am, I Can, I Will. But don't think I know all the answers," he said, running his fingers along a strip of blond-colored cedar. "I'll only disappoint you if you put your trust in me. You have to trust yourself."

"Why are you building a kayak, anyway?" I asked him.

He turned and looked at me. "Why?"

"Yeah."

"I'm going to ask you to think about that question for a moment, Milo."

"Think about it?"

"Yes. Just think about it. Take as long as you need to think about it."

I realized I must have asked something really stupid and this was Dad's way of making me see it. But why *was* he building a kayak? That wasn't a stupid question, was it? And besides, stupid question or not, there *was* an answer, right? So maybe it wasn't so much a stupid question as it was a question that had an obvious answer.

What was the obvious answer to the question "Why are you building a kayak?"

Possible answers: Because the Cog had told him to? Because he wanted to? Why *not* build a kayak? The sweet smell of the wood and the glue, the scratch of the sandpaper. This object taking shape, actually becoming a kayak. Yes! That was the answer. It *was* obvious. Dad was building a kayak *to build a kayak*!

Noticing the smile that had come onto my face, Dad smiled back at me. He tapped his forehead. "The Cog," he said in a very deep voice. "I *told* you the vibrational intensity around here was incredible, didn't I?"

"I think I feel it!" I said.

"Trust yourself. That is the Cog. The Cog merely unlocks the door that lets you in. The Cog is an instrument, a tool, just like any of these tools around us."

"How can I make sense out of my life?" I asked.

"The same way you made sense out of the kayak."

I nodded, but I must have looked confused, because

Dad said, "Don't think too much, Milo. That's the worst form of resistance. You don't have to think here in Arizona. You don't have to analyze anything when you're building a kayak. You don't have to ask why or how. Just let it sink in. If you start thinking too much and getting confused, then just remember the Cog: I Am, I Can, I Will."

• • •

The next day we drove out to some old churches and Spanish missions hidden away in the hills. Dad knew the age of most of the buildings and what kind of materials they were made out of. It reminded me of the old brick barbecue in our backyard, and that made me sad, especially when the sun went down.

That night, my second one in Arizona, I had trouble sleeping. I was using the sofa in the sitting room for a bed. My head was burning, my face was all sweaty, and my heart was racing. I knew I'd been having a dream, but the moment I opened my eyes and remembered I was in Arizona, I couldn't recall any of it.

I got out of bed and put on my shoes and went outside into the yard. The air smelled sharp and prickly like cacti, full of the nighttime noises of toads and insects. And the stars—the stars were a big whoosh, this smear of bright lights all across the sky, and the rock hills glowed from the starlight.

My mind was quiet and still. I felt sad. Part of it might

have been homesickness. Part of it was that I didn't want to disappoint my dad. My brain just could not grasp the Cog. It was beyond me. I needed something solid, something I could touch and smell, like the kayak. It was a horrible thing to admit, but maybe I didn't care about concepts and ideas and philosophies. Maybe I just cared about . . . things?

• • •

My last day in Arizona, Dad and I drove to Sedona, where I met his new lady friend, Tawny. She was very cool. I mean, she had this wisdom that seemed to radiate from her. I wondered if it was the Cog.

Tawny had spent twenty-four years on the road touring as a backup singer with the Pappy Durango Band. She'd been everywhere and done everything. She'd finally retired from the music scene and bought a little arts-and-crafts shop in Sedona. She wore a New York Yankees baseball cap—sometimes facing the right way and sometimes turned around backward. Her hair was braided and she smoked cigars. She was thin, like a dancer, and her face had this tough wrinkly wisdom. She didn't wear any makeup. She seemed a lot older than Dad, but they appeared to get along pretty well—when they weren't arguing.

We had dinner at a fancy restaurant. Dad ordered braised antelope, and I was going to ask him when he had started eating red meat, but I let it go. He and Tawny started bickering about some trivial thing for the next five minutes.

When she went outside to smoke a cigar, I said to Dad, "She's a pretty nice lady."

Dad said, "I know you mean well, but I try not to pass judgment on others. We're always putting ourselves in a position of judging others as 'nice' or 'good' or 'weird' or whatever. We need to just accept them for whoever they are and not label them. There are times when Tawny is a real bitch. Trust me on that . . . So tell me more about this Stephen Yamashita guy."

"What do you want to know?"

"He's Japanese, I take it?"

"Pretty much. Not entirely."

"He has children?"

"Yeah. Three of them. A boy and two girls. I haven't met them yet."

"Why haven't you met them?"

"I don't know. There's some sort of a grand plan. But I don't know what it is."

"He's pretty well off?"

"You mean loaded? Rich?"

"Yes. I ask that simply as a way of better understanding his type. I don't place any particular importance or respect on people with money. But it does help me to get a better idea of their type."

"Mom won't say how rich he is. She says he's comfortable. He dresses pretty well. And Shan says they've been talking about a prenup."

Dad smiled fondly. "Good old Shan. There's one bitch I do not miss at all."

• • •

I had a hard time saying goodbye to Dad at the airport. I guess it must have been jet lag or something. I felt like I was going to cry. The trip seemed to have ended too quickly. We'd gotten some good work done on the kayak, but Dad still had many hours ahead of him before it would be ready to launch in a river. I wondered when I would see him again.

"It'd be great to try out that kayak when it's finished," I said.

"I'll plant a seed for you to come and visit for an entire week," he said. "Let's see, this is March now. When do you get out of school?"

"Sometime in June," I said.

"June," he said, rubbing his beard. "June . . ."

He must have been planting a mental seed.

"Maybe the Cog can help," I said.

He looked at me. "We plant the seed, we water it, we nurture it, but we can't make it grow."

"No," I said.

"Life makes it grow," he said. "Life happens to it. Growth happens to it. We can't see it happening with our eyes."

"Right," I said.

"Milo, I'm going to tell you something. I believe you're ready for it."

I was listening. I was listening with all my might. We were standing near where the line to go through security formed.

"I've already told you there's only one path to the Cog, and that's the path of least resistance. But there's something I haven't told you. There really is no path at all."

"How can that be?" I said.

"Imagine the vast desert. Or a mountain meadow full of grass and flowers. When you walk across the desert or meadow, you don't need to follow any path. All you need to do is walk. Nobody can tell you what direction to go or what path to follow. You have to find out as you go. Nobody can lead you. The direction is entirely up to you. Because the meadow isn't something separate from you. Dude, you *are* the meadow."

• • •

Well, I said goodbye to Dad more confused than ever. The path of least resistance had been something I could sort of understand. But now, at the very last minute, he tells me there is no path, that I am the meadow. Strange. Yet when I boarded the airplane to Seattle, I felt calm and my senses were alert. I didn't feel as though I needed to come up with any synonyms for how I felt about Dad or his philosophy. I sat in the window seat and buckled up. The plane taxied and took off, and soon we were flying over the desert.

My dad was down there somewhere in the desert, but

part of him was still in me. I was taking my dad with me. I was taking the kayak with me, too, and the desert, that too. How long would they last in me? Hopefully, until I went back for another visit.

Then it hit me once again that I didn't seem to care about concepts. That maybe I wasn't really a seeker of truth like my dad was. That I didn't care about finding enlightenment or the Cog. Wouldn't have cared about the Cog even if it came up and bit me in the ass.

Maybe the only thing I'd ever been seeking was this feeling of my dad's presence in me.

When Mom picked me up at the airport, she looked at me for a long time, and I wondered if she could see a change.

"You look great," she said. "Three days in the sun, my, my."

"Arizona is a very mystical place," I said.

Mom went pale. "He didn't give you drugs, did he?"

"No!"

She asked me a lot of questions during the drive home from the airport. I knew she wanted me to give her all the details of my visit, but I really didn't feel like getting into a bunch of girl talk with her. I wasn't her girlfriend.

But she insisted I at least tell her something that was a high point—what was my favorite thing about Arizona?

"The kayak," I said without hesitating. "I helped him work on the kayak he's building."

Mom didn't seem too thrilled by that answer. She just said something like "Oh, that's nice."

# 20

wait–anticipation–expectancy–certainty–
confidence–inevitability–fate–fortune–wealth–
abundance–leftovers

Through the rest of March and on past my birthday, I waited to hear from my dad. I wrote him a letter telling him to be sure and keep me up-to-date on that kayak and the seed he'd planted.

April was a hectic month. Stephen and my mother were making twice-a-week trips to the pair of therapists.

That's right, twice a week.

I asked my mom how much the therapists cost per hour. I was just curious, thinking maybe, what, fifty, seventy-five dollars an hour?

When she told me, I knew I hadn't heard it right, or else she'd misunderstood my question.

"No," I said. "How much *per hour*."

"That's what it is," she said. "Per hour."

"No, it isn't."

"Yes, it is. That's the going rate."

"That can't be. You have to be kidding me. This is some kind of mind trick you're playing with me."

"Milo. That's what it is. You can go ahead and stand there and gape. I've got laundry to do." She started to walk away, then hesitated. "Would you like to have a session with them sometime?"

"A session . . . You mean talk to them?"

"Yeah."

"What about?"

"Whatever's on your mind. Maybe stuff you don't want to talk to me about."

"Do they analyze you?"

"I don't know, I suppose they do. Why?"

"Analyzing and thinking just get in your way," I said. "They're just forms of resistance."

"Hm. Well, that's an interesting theory. I'm sure they'd be interested to hear it. Why don't you give it some thought? They'd really like to sit down with you for an hour."

She headed toward the pantry.

I stood there. *One hour* with their therapists cost as much as one Trail Tiger 300 TZ motorbike. For every hour they spent with their therapists, they could have bought a brand-new Trail Tiger 300 TZ motorbike.

There was no possible way any therapists could be

worth that, unless maybe they hypnotized you or something.

It was weird to think about how much I had begged Mom for that motorbike two years ago. It was hard to remember that far back.

I followed her into the pantry. "Is Stephen paying for it?"

"For what?"

"The therapists."

"Yes."

"Well, he wouldn't pay for me, too, would he?"

"Sure he would."

"Man." I shook my head. "What does he do again? I mean for work."

She looked up from her basket of dirty clothes. "Well, it's fascinating, really. It's really interesting work. He owns a lot of businesses."

"That's pretty fascinating. Is that what you like best about him, that he's rich?"

"No. I like him because he's . . . he's smart. He's gentle. He's humble. He's classy. He's funny. He makes me feel secure when I'm with him."

"Do you love him?"

Mom thought about it for a couple of seconds. "Yes."

"Are you going to marry him?"

She paused again. "We've talked about it. We're just at the talking stage. I mean, there are so many things to work out. Like where we'd live. That's a big one. I won't live in his dead wife's house. I refused to do that. But Stephen and his kids are very attached to that house. He and Mega-beth put so much work into it. And you haven't even met his children yet. I'm still trying to arrange that dinner. It's a major feat trying to work around Fawn and Lyric's soccer schedule."

"So just double-checking—if you do marry him, you're not just marrying him for his money?"

"No."

"You mentioned it once."

"I know. I remember."

"But you took it back."

"That's right."

"I'm just making sure."

Mom smiled. "I know. You're watching out for me. You are so growing up. You're a good kid, you know that? I'm glad you had fun with your father. It's good for you to spend time together." Mom's eyes started filling up with tears. "You'll have a chance to get to know Stephen better, too. Stephen's an excellent judge of character, and he really likes you."

"Does he have a strong character?"

"Stephen? Yes, I'd say he has a very strong character."

"Would you say Dad has a weak one?"

"I'd say he's got a major character flaw. He's all wrapped up in his own personal growth, yet he's never grown up. He doesn't behave like a grownup. Your grandpa tried to warn me."

"Grandpa Rom?"

"Yeah, he tried to talk me out of marrying your dad. Being a coach all those years, he knew how to read a boy's character. He sat me down and said he respected Luke's intelligence but he felt Luke had a lot of growing up left to do and that he'd never done a real day's work in his life. I'd always worshipped my father, but I didn't listen to him. Your grandpa never said another word about it. He accepted Luke as my husband and your father, and they had a cordial relationship."

• • •

Mom found out from Stephen what his kids would eat: spaghetti and tomato sauce. The night they were coming over, I asked Mom to tell me more about this Tarquillin kid. I'd been mentally keeping a running list of all the words and phrases she'd used to describe him:

Different
IQ of a genius
Looking for ways to channel all of his brilliance
Tense

Personally, I thought it was a scary list. It was even scarier to think that this guy and I could possibly end up being stepbrothers and sharing a house.

"All right," Mom said. "I'll tell you a story about Tarquillin. Stephen told me this story the other day. He swears it's the absolute truth. Want to hear it?"

"Sure."

Stephen's wife, Beth, was driving in the car with the three kids. Tarquillin was six years old at the time, Lyric and Fawn were three and four. Beth had taken the kids to visit some relatives in northern Idaho for Thanksgiving. Stephen hadn't been able to come because he'd had to go away on business.

So Beth and the kids spent Thanksgiving with the Idaho relatives, who lived way out in the middle of nowhere, and when they were driving home, Beth decided to take a shortcut and made a couple of wrong turns, and they ended up lost on a country road, with nothing around for miles and miles. Nothing.

All of a sudden, they get a flat tire.

So here's Beth, out in the middle of nowhere, with these three kids six and under, and a flat tire. She tries her cell phone, but there's no signal. Nothing. No cars have passed by. What's she going to do? Change the tire, right? So she gets out the spare tire, and she jacks up the car and starts taking off the lug nuts. Only there's a problem. She's only able to get two lug nuts off. The other two are on too tight. Whoever put them on last had overtightened them, and now it was impossible for Beth to loosen them. Meanwhile it's getting dark and cold, and they're lost, and there's no sign of any cars.

Beth is starting to panic.

But little Tarquillin, six years old, says, "Mother, do we have any emergency flares?"

"Yes, we do, but who's going to see them? It's not dark yet. And we can't waste them. There are no houses or cars for us to signal."

"Mother, get one of the road flares."

Beth goes and gets one out of the kit in the trunk.

"What are you going to do, set off a flare for help?"

"Of course."

"But, honey, I just told you—"

He set off the flare. But instead of dropping it on the ground, he held it up to the lug nuts.

In less than a minute, the heat from the flare loosened the lug nuts so that Beth was able to get them off and put on the spare tire, and eventually they found their way back to the main highway and drove home.

I guessed I'd have to meet the kid for myself to decide whether I believed that story, but it sure sounded like a myth.

• • •

Fawn and Lyric were a couple of very cute girls, and soccer was their religion. As for the flare guy, Tarquillin, the first thing I noticed about him was that he had these delicate hands and long fingernails. They were professional nose-picking fingernails. During dinner I could not stop imagining him using those long fingernails to extract juicy green boogers from inside his nose. He was a few weeks away from turning fourteen, which made him fourteen months younger than me, but the way he acted, he seemed like a student at Oxford or something. Everything he said was a downer. Things like "We're all slaves to conformity" and "There is no escape from our bondage except total annihilation of all that we know" and "Our civilization is going to destroy itself; the human race will be extinct in fifteen years."

"Tarquillin, is your spaghetti okay?" Mom asked him. He had taken only a couple bites of it.

He said he was writing a play about the devil. He was writing a lot of poetry, too.

"About the devil, right?" I said.

"About marigolds."

After dinner, we split up into two parties. Mom, Stephen, and the two girls played a board game. I invited Tarquillin to come and hang out in my room until it was time for dessert.

He examined the odds and ends that I'd collected over the years. My books, my computer, my football trophies and plaques. He picked up a picture of my dad and me and looked at it for a long time. He flipped through my book of synonyms and read the inscription from Ms. Swinford.

"Charming." He snapped the book shut.

He sat down in my desk chair and I sat on the edge of my bed.

"It's going to drive her nuts that you didn't eat her

spaghetti," I said. "Things like that sort of bother my mom. Once, she stayed up half the night making a coffee cake for your dad."

"Nothing personal," he said. "It's not every day I get a chance to meet a *Milo*. I didn't want to distract myself with food. We observe these useless rituals, like 'eating together.' Why do we have to 'eat together'? We don't shower together. We don't take a crap together. Yet for some reason we feel we have to be in each other's presence when we ingest protein and carbohydrates."

Amazing. Here was a guy who might be more antisocial than I was.

"I don't get out much," he added, as if there might have been some doubt about that.

"What do you do?" I said.

"Spend most of the time in my workshop."

"What do you do in your workshop?"

"I can't tell you that."

"You'd have to kill me?"

He rubbed his face with his hands. "I'm worn out. This evening has been a strain on me. I don't have the energy to answer any more questions right now."

"Maybe you should have eaten more spaghetti," I said.

# 21

step–advance–progress–climb–scale–
hike–plod–stagger–trip–misstep

Mom and Stephen (and their therapists) must have thought the meeting of the children was a definite step forward. Stephen had even taken his kids to see the therapists. They had all agreed they'd be willing to move out of their house into a brand-new one, as long as it was still within a ten-mile radius of Fawn and Lyric's soccer club.

I never would have believed it, but I guessed my mom wanted to marry Stephen more than she wanted to live in Seattle, because she asked me how I felt about the prospect of moving out to the suburbs.

I thought about the path of least resistance. I thought about Arizona, and wondered if my dad was going to invite me back this summer.

I had been in a holding pattern ever since I'd returned from Arizona. Hopping on buses and riding them around to different neighborhoods after school had become sort of stale. As the weather got nicer, I pictured myself as some lone pathetic guy who rode buses around. The buses had started to get downright depressing. Pretty soon I would cross the line and become one of the smelly passengers who muttered to himself. I'd grow my fingernails long just so I could pick my nose better.

So what if I were to move again? New house. New school. New football team. New family.

Maybe I was ready to give up the bus riding.

Way out in the suburbs, out where Stephen and his kids lived, nobody rode buses. Everybody drove.

I saw myself behind the wheel of my own car. I could enter tenth grade with a new identity. No one would know me. I could reinvent myself. I could change my look—I could be more clean-cut or dirty-cut. I could be a nerd or a jock. I could be a hardworking studious student or goof-off like there was no tomorrow. I could be a clean slate. I could be the hero or the villain of my own story.

"I'm in," I said to my mom.

• • •

One evening I was in the living room in front of the TV with my homework spread out on the coffee table, when Stephen came in. I quickly changed the channel because I had been watching a cheerleading competition.

Stephen had that look on his face that said, Must Execute Man-to-Man Talk. My mom had warned me this might be coming. I noticed she was nowhere around.

He cleared his throat. "Mind if we talk for a minute, Milo?"

I turned off the TV.

He sat down at the other end of the couch.

He cleared his throat again.

He started to make a speech about what a "special lady" my mom was and how when they got married and we all moved in together we would all . . .

I was still thinking about the cheerleading competition.

I had stumbled on it while I'd been channel flipping. Just before Stephen had come in, a team of cheerleaders from LaFayette, Georgia, had formed a human pyramid. The last and lightest girl had climbed to the top of the pyramid. Her uniform was a different color than the others'—theirs were purple and hers was all white, so when she climbed to the top she looked like a patch of snow on a dark mountain. She stood there grinning to the world with her arms in a V.

All I could do was marvel at this. A bunch of cheerleaders had turned themselves into a snowcapped mountain.

Stephen was still giving his speech. When he finally got done I said, "Sounds all right to me."

He seemed surprised and then relieved. He was probably wondering if it qualified as a real man-to-man talk if only one man had done all the talking.

He cleared his throat again. "Uh, anything in particular

you'd like to ask me? Anything at all that you'd like to get off your chest?"

"No, not really," I said.

"Good enough. Anytime you ever want to—"

"I have a question."

"Excellent."

"How did you become a success in life? What's your secret?"

"Hard work. Going the extra mile. Luck."

"What do you actually do for a living?"

"I own businesses. I hire the right people to run them."

"So you're your own boss?"

"Yep."

"You don't actually do any of the work yourself?"

"Nope. I've reached a certain point where—because I worked my butt off and paid my dues—it sort of runs itself. It's kind of like playing Monopoly. Once you're all set up with your property, people just go around and around the board and you collect your money."

I shook my head in wonder. "Is it something you could teach somebody? Or do they have to be a genius?"

"Believe me, Milo, I'm no genius. As a matter of fact, I dropped out of college. I went out and got my education in the real world. As I've told Tarquillin many times—though I'm not sure he actually agrees with it—a genius is just somebody who's willing to be totally obsessed by whatever he's doing. I don't know if it's something that can be taught. But I do believe it's something that can be learned—if you're willing."

• • •

A few days after that, Stephen gave me a stack of books and told me to take a look at any or all of them and we could discuss them in the coming weeks. The books were mostly about money and investing, and how to play the game of making more money. Some of them were kind of philosophical, and they talked about the quest for wealth the same way my dad used to talk about the quest for truth. Several times I meant to look up *wealth* in my synonym book, but I never got around to it.

Toward the end of May, Mom and I went on another camping trip. This time we drove up into Canada.

We bundled up in front of the campfire and drank some concoction of wildflower tea from tin cups. Mom had put a little bit of wine in the tea and I felt a twinkling in my head. I'd been reading one of Stephen's books during much of the long drive, and my head was full of fantasies about being a budding entrepreneur. Now I looked over at my mom and said, "Are you going to quit your job when you guys get married?"

"Good God, I hope not. We'll have to see. Three years of working my butt off to get that certificate? But I'm also thinking about having some quality time with you. And Stephen, too, of course. Both of you."

"And his three kids?"

"Yeah, them, too."

"Did you sign a prenup?"

"Yeah."

I nodded sagely.

"Do you think money is God?" I said.

"What?"

"Do you think money is God."

"No. Why, do you?"

"Yes."

"Why would you think that?"

"It's the solution to every problem of life," I said. "It's like a magic wand. It gives you all kinds of power, it makes you healthier because you can afford to eat better, it makes you more comfortable, it makes you less stressed out, better educated, better looking. It sets you free. You can travel, go anywhere you want to go, first class all the way."

In the glow of the campfire I could feel my mom studying me as if she was trying to look inside me.

"There's something wrong with that theory of yours," she said, "but I'm not smart enough to say what it is. It's a trick argument. If it were true, then all the rich people would be blissfully happy. But there are plenty of miserable rich people."

"That's just because they go overboard with it. They get greedy."

"I don't really think you believe money is God."

"If you and Dad had been rich, you never would have gotten divorced. We'd still be living in our house."

"I don't know if that's true. I really don't. Is that what your dad told you?"

"No. But you fought about money a lot."

"He was also having a fling with one of his students."

"That's not what you were fighting about. That didn't even come out until after he left. You were fighting about money. If you had won the lottery or something, you would have been able to change whatever you didn't like about your life, and you wouldn't have had anything to fight about, and you would have stayed together. Money would have kept you together."

Mom didn't say anything for a minute. When she did, her voice sounded weary. "Yeah, well, we didn't win the lottery. And if you think winning the lottery is the same as finding God and solving all your problems, then you're a fool."

"That's just what all the rich people want the losers to keep on believing," I said. "The tycoons want you to believe money can't buy happiness, and that way you won't try to get rich, and they won't have any competition. You'll be happy being their servant and working for them."

"Where did you pick this theory up?"

"A little here, a little there. Actually, Stephen gave me a few books to read."

"Well, then, I guess the way you'll find out for sure is to get rich. How do you plan on doing that?"

"I don't know. I'll figure something out."

"God. You remind me so much of your father. You both talk utter crap but I can't outargue either one of you. Look, I'll tell you how to get rich. Stephen'll back me up on this. Networking. That's it. That's the key. Knowing people. Meeting people. Making contacts. The more people you know, the more opportunities present themselves."

I wanted to ask her something, but I didn't want to hurt her feelings. But I asked it anyway.

"How come you didn't follow your own advice?" I said.

"What?"

"I mean, you talk about how important networking is. Why did you choose dental tech instead of something where you could go out and schmooze and network? That's what you're really good at. You could have been a salesman or something."

Mom sat back and looked at the fire, and I was afraid I had hurt her feelings. "That's a very good point," she said. "You're right. It's my own fault. I was crazy. I was going through a divorce; we were broke. I listened to some two-bit life coach that my mother and Shan hired for me. It was a mistake. The whole three years. Sometimes that's the way I feel about my whole adult life. Mistake, mistake, mistake."

She seemed to think about this for a minute, and then she added, "But, of course, you came out of it, so it wasn't a complete disaster."

I smiled. "I'm touched."

She shook her head and laughed quietly.

During the drive home, she asked me if I'd given any more thought to having a session with her therapists. I said I didn't see how they could possibly be worth all that money they charged, but I'd see them.

"But only under one condition," I said. "If they say the word *network* or tell me I need to join a club, I'm going to walk out. I can get that advice for free."

"That's a deal," she said.

# 22

horizon–prospect–scenery–panorama–
picture–image–apparition–ghost

Summer vacation was on the horizon; still no word from Dad.

Mom and Stephen were spending all their time house-hunting in their chosen area. They hired a realtor named Lonnie Bunchway, who had gone to their high school but had graduated two years ahead of them. Lonnie would call Mom at least once a day and tell her she'd found the perfect house, and Mom would drop everything and go look at it.

Ditta was taking our leaving pretty hard. She put a FOR RENT sign out front and showed our place to potential renters. Her cats didn't seem to care one way or the other.

On a rainy May afternoon I took a bus to the therapists'

office in a small building on Westlake Avenue, overlooking Lake Union.

I was a little nervous, not sure of what they might unearth from inside my head. They were probably experts at digging around in your brain, and if they dug deep enough I was sure they'd find plenty of things wrong with me.

They had me sit down in a comfortable leather chair with my back to them, facing a poster, so that I wouldn't be distracted by having to make eye contact. Their names were Kevin and Karen. They were a true team. Not only were they partners, they were husband and wife. They sat side by side, taking turns finishing each other's sentences.

The poster in front of me was a photograph of a mountain. Trees in the foreground, red and yellow flowers on a slope, patches of snow in the background, the mountain beyond capped with snow.

"Is that in the Swiss Alps?" I asked.

"Actually, no, it's Mount Baker," they said. "That's in our state. The state of Washington."

Okay, now that they had established my IQ . . .

"Milo, we'd like to try something. We'd like to explore a little and see if we can get to the heart of what you really want. We're not too interested in the past. In fact, we'd like to just leave the past out of it completely. Let's start from the present. Our job is not necessarily to help you get what you want, but to help you identify it. To help you *look* at it. Does that make sense?"

"Look at it?"

"Yes."

"Okay." There was a long pause. I thought maybe they were waiting for me to say something. Their voices seemed to have had a lulling effect on me.

After a while I said, "Uh . . . are you waiting for me to tell you what I want?"

"Do you know what you want?"

I was going to mention something about truth or wealth, but for some reason, I couldn't say anything. I couldn't even make a sound. I wondered if they'd secretly hypnotized me. If they had, they were worth every dollar they charged.

"How about if you just sit back and close your eyes, Milo. Relax. Breathe in, breathe out. Don't worry, you won't fall asleep."

"Are you going to hypnotize me?"

"No."

"Oh." I was a bit disappointed.

"We're going to ask you to tell us a story. We'd like to hear the story of a young man named Milo Bastion. Start with the marriage of Cori Bastion and Stephen Yamashita and take it from there. Where do you see that story going? Just go with it. Try not to think about it or ask why."

I was glad they added that, because I didn't see what this had to do with what I wanted. "Go with it?" I said. "All right. I'll try that."

I sat back in my comfortable chair. I could almost hear my dad saying, *You're the protagonist of your own life story.*

I closed my eyes.

"Uh, once upon a time," I said, "Cori and Stephen got married. They moved into a new house. It was a big enough house so that Milo Bastion didn't have to share a bathroom with anybody."

I paused, and listened to Kevin and Karen both scribbling away. I didn't know what words were going to come out of my mouth. *Don't think,* I told myself. I continued.

"They bought him a car when he turned sixteen. A convertible. No, make it an SUV, four-wheel drive. So he could drive it up into the mountains and go hiking.

"So one day he drives up there for a hike, he's hiking this trail. He's got his knapsack with his lunch in it. The trail climbs through timber and goes along a ridge that looks out over the valley. He sees some hikers every now and then and he waves his hat to them, and they wave back to him. The sun is shining and the sky is deep blue, with a few clouds. Chipmunks scurry around. Crows caw. Marmots squeak. There's a hushed sound of wind in the treetops. The trail keeps going up into blue sky. The sky is so blue, he feels like he can touch it. Along comes this girl, hiking alone. She's hiking all by herself. She stops and they talk for a while. They have good sex.

"Eventually Milo graduates from high school. He decides to do some traveling. He goes to Switzerland. He sees Lucerne, Montreux, Bern, Geneva, Zermatt, and all the little villages in between. He hikes the Swiss Alps, scales the Matterhorn. On the slopes of the Matterhorn he meets a Swiss girl. She knows all of Europe really well, and speaks several languages, and they travel around Europe together and meet interesting people, network, have adventures.

"But eventually he goes back home and goes to college and he gets a general well-rounded education and reads philosophy and classics, but he also learns about business so that he knows the secret of making money, and he also builds things with his hands—he's a craftsman *and* a scholar *and* his own boss. When he gets out of college he is completely free and totally alive, and he's astounded by life. That's it, he kind of *marvels* at life. He laughs a lot, he finds himself cracking up out loud quite often. He does whatever he pleases and everything pleases him. Eventually he dies. That's the end."

There was a long silence. Kevin and Karen were writing. I opened my eyes and took in the view of the mountain poster.

Finally, they said, "That was very interesting. Tell us, Milo, what do you think is the least believable part of the story you just told?"

"The good sex."

They wrote some more.

I waited for my mind to start thinking again. I don't know how much time passed. Pretty soon I noticed that the room was still and quiet. The scribbling had stopped. My eyes were open, staring into nothing but space.

"What are you thinking?" they asked.

The mountains. Travel. Getting away. The truth.

I'd never traveled anywhere except Arizona. I had really enjoyed the traveling part of that, every leg of the trip. Even sitting in the airport and being on the plane. The idea of going somewhere, being on a journey. Those buses I rode around to different neighborhoods. But that's in the past. And in fifth grade, that song called "The Happy Wanderer." That's in the past, too. That kid in the song isn't me, never was.

I'm not sure how much of this I said to myself and how much I said out loud. Maybe I really was hypnotized and didn't know whether I was talking, thinking, or muttering.

But now I could see why Kevin and Karen charged so much money. They were good, amazingly good. They made me do all the work, that's how good they were.

• • •

In June, Mom and Stephen found a house that was pretty close to what they considered perfect. It also happened to be practically a mansion. They bought it. I was definitely not going to have to share a bathroom.

In July they got married in Stephen and Megabeth's old house, which had a FOR SALE sign in the front yard. It was a small ceremony, just a little family gathering. Me and Aunt Shan and Grandma Nordquist and Ditta. Stephen's kids. Stephen's younger brother from Colorado. That was it. After the ceremony came the champagne. After the champagne, the big feast. Then Mom and Stephen left on an eight-day honeymoon cruise to Alaska. I went home with Grandma Nordquist and stayed with her for three days. For the other five days, I stayed on my own. I had Ditta upstairs looking in on me, and Aunt Shan came and hung out with me at night and helped me pack up my stuff and label boxes for our move.

Mom and Stephen were due back from their honeymoon on Sunday. So on Saturday I took a bus to my old neighborhood. There were lots of people out for a stroll, many of them walking dogs or jogging. The air was full of the sounds of lawn mowers and the smell of mown grass. I wondered if I'd run into anybody I knew, any of my old friends, maybe one of the guys who had come to our going-away potluck. Maybe I had changed so much since we'd lived here that I had grown unrecognizable.

I turned the corner and came to our old house. I couldn't tell if anybody was home, but I didn't care, I went around the side of the house and had a look at the backyard. The brick barbecue was still there. It still smelled like charcoal, with a hint of my dad's pipe.

I walked the six blocks to my elementary school. Stepping into the flower bed, I peered in the window of what used to be Ms. Swinford's classroom. I imagined the way it used to look inside, the desk configuration, the cuckoo clock, the bulletin board and seasonal wall decorations. I could almost smell the floor varnish and the sudsy stuff we squirted on our desks every Friday when we cleaned them off with paper towels and made them shiny. I imagined me and the other handful of teacher's pets sitting around Ms. Swinford's classroom listening to the music of the Swiss and Bavarian Alps.

I hoped she had made it back to Switzerland. That was where she belonged. Either that, or back in her hometown, Wenatchee.

I stared at my reflection in the window. I made a couple of faces, just so I knew it was really me. Then I pressed my forehead against the cold glass and closed my eyes. I listened as all the external sounds faded and silence came in. That's when I heard her voice. It came through the window. It was muffled, so I couldn't make out any actual words, but I could hear the tone of Ms. Swinford's voice, the music of it, and it sounded so happy and close to me. It gave me goose pimples all over my arms. I could feel her presence with me. I wondered if it was her ghost. For the first time, it occurred to me that she might have died. That's why I was feeling her presence so powerfully. Maybe losing her teaching job had been such a blow that she'd had an accident or gotten some fatal illness or . . . who knows.

But my imagination was getting carried away. I needed to snap out of it. Ms. Swinford had always expected good things, always made others happy. She had the love of her family in Wenatchee. She had Aunt Liesl and Uncle Cedric. I shouldn't think the worst about her. I knew that all I had to do was remember her as she was, and then she'd never change, she'd always be like that. I shouldn't have come back here. It was a bad idea. I should have kept the classroom in my memory. Maybe if I really concentrated, I could go through the window into the classroom on the other side, and I'd be in fifth grade again, and Ms. Swinford would be there, and I could just live in there and not come out, like Virginia in the cuckoo clock.

# Tenth Grade

# 23

move–relocate–evacuate–pass–discharge–
send forth–set in motion–drive–chauffeur

We merged our families and moved into the new mega-house in the middle of August. The house was out in the foothills of the Cascade Mountains, bordered by dense critter-filled woods that would never be touched by developers or made into "Phase 2."

One of the most stunning features of our new house was that it had six bathrooms. Tarquillin and I each had one of our own. The two girls shared another one. Mom and Stephen had one in their master suite. That made four. The guest bathroom downstairs made five. There was a mysterious sixth one between the garage and the laundry room for "hired laborers."

Another feature was the five-hundred-foot driveway.

Two or three years ago I would have sold my soul to spend a day puttering up and down my own private driveway on a little motorbike. Instead, I spent what was left of the summer running down that driveway and along the hilly forest road to get in shape for football and girls. Mostly football. My mom had made it clear: You want a car for your sixteenth birthday, you play a sport or find something else to join. Or no car.

So I turned out for the football team. Football at my new high school was a totally different experience for me. In the past, football had been fun, more or less. Now it was a job. It was hard work just to make the team. There were so many people turning out that they had to cut thirty bodies by the end of the first week. I worked my ass off, because I didn't want to face the humiliation of getting cut, and I didn't want to have to find something else to join in order to get a car. But it was tough. There were some big kids and heavy hitters, guys whose fathers were ex-college or ex-pro players, guys who'd gone to football camp every summer.

Somehow, I made the team. Which meant I had earned the chance to get the crap knocked out of me every day in practice. For the month of September I had a permanent limp, and my mom was sympathetic.

I made the varsity squad as a second-string defensive end, but I sat on the bench most of the time. Still, it was varsity, and that meant I didn't have to be a social outcast at school if I didn't want to be.

Life was easy at that school. It should have been called Least Resistance High. It was like an expensive resort or country club nestled in acres of woods. The buildings on the campus all looked like log cabins on the outside, and on the inside the temperature was kept at a comfortable 68 degrees, no matter what the weather was like. The walkways between buildings were heated, glass-enclosed, and carpeted. There were two student parking lots filled with late-model cars and trucks. Some of the cafeteria food was prepared by students who were taking gourmet cooking as an elective.

There were plenty of girls at school who looked very attractive to me, and I fell in love with many of them that fall. I thought about asking someone to one of the dances, but I figured I'd wait until April when I got my driver's license—and, hopefully, a car.

So I kept to myself most of the time.

I wasn't lonely, I preferred myself as a companion. But still, it was kind of weird how I had naturally slipped back into my solitary ways. I was the same old Milo I'd always been. Maybe it's just not possible to reinvent yourself, no matter how many times you start over in a new school.

• • •

One day I came home from football practice and found Tarquillin in my bathroom. He was sitting on the toilet reading a magazine. The smell staggered me.

"What's up?" I said, holding my breath.

"Not a whole lot." He turned a page of the magazine.

"What are you doing?" I tried not to sound hostile or threatening, just mildly curious.

"Relaxing over a recent bowel movement," he said. He turned another page.

"Is there something wrong with your toilet?" I couldn't quite believe we were having this conversation.

"No," he said. "Look, if you'd rather I didn't . . ." His voice trailed off.

I shrugged. "I was just wondering what the point is."

"Point?" He reached for the toilet paper and started to unroll a handful. That was it for me—I wasn't going to stick around and watch him.

When I mentioned it to my mom, she just said that Tarquillin was testing the concepts of space and boundaries.

"Maybe you'd better keep your bedroom door locked for a while," she said.

• • •

I liked Fawn and Lyric. Being so close in age, they were on the same soccer team—the same select team with the same group of girls year after year. Their team played in games and leagues and tournaments all over. It took up all their time. That simplified their lives quite a bit.

My life was pretty simple, too. I'd made it through football season, and now I was counting the days till I hit sixteen and got my driver's license.

Amazingly, Mom and Stephen still acted like newly-weds. They still held hands and gave each other back rubs and kissed goodbye and hello. Sometimes I'd see them standing out in the backyard, arms around each other, gazing at the sweeping territorial view, with the mountains in the background, or gazing at each other. They were so into each other it didn't matter what they gazed at. When it started raining they'd duck under the gazebo and make out.

Stephen ran his various businesses from his home office or, when the weather got better, from the golf course. He seemed to have a lot of friends, and they all had hearty laughs and would grab Mom and kiss her on the cheek and laugh some more. They'd look at me with merry eyes and hearty good-natured red-faced manliness that reminded me of so many of my old coaches and Scout leaders.

Mom, as usual, had made plenty of new friends in our area. In January she'd quit her job at the lab and become a full-time stay-at-home mother. She started a book club, took piano lessons, and went to Seattle to visit her friends there. In February she joined a women's indoor soccer league.

She usually cooked dinner, and at least once or twice a week she'd try to have all six of us sit at the dining room table for dinner at the same time—usually spaghetti and tomato sauce. Sometimes she would light candles.

Even Tarquillin had to sit at the table for those family dinners, keeping his arms pressed to his sides so that he didn't rub elbows with anybody while we did our ingesting.

During one of those spaghetti dinners, my mom and Stephen were having a discussion about money. They were throwing around phrases like "world currency" and "foreign oil" and "geopolitical domination," and at one point I think they said the word *money* about five times in one sentence.

I couldn't follow what they were talking about, and Fawn and Lyric weren't even listening. But Tarquillin, he'd been listening intently to them. I waited to see what he was going to say. But he said nothing. Keeping his expression utterly blank, he reached into his back pocket, took out his wallet, removed a twenty-dollar bill from it, and lit the bill on fire with a candle. My mom and Stephen stopped talking. Fawn and Lyric looked at each other and rolled their eyes. I watched the whole bill burn right down to his long fingernails before he dropped the ashes on his plate of spaghetti. As usual, whatever point he'd been trying to make was over my head, but it occurred to me that he might be the devil, because I still kind of thought money was God.

• • •

The winter days went by slowly. Every chance I got, I took the car out with Mom or Stephen and practiced driving. Here I was, once again in a holding pattern, waiting for the future. I'd been doing that all my life, always waiting for something in the future to hurry up and get here so that things would be different and I could really start to live.

Maybe one of these days in the future I'd figure out how to stop waiting for the future.

Mom asked me if I wanted to pay another visit to Kevin and Karen, but I said no, I didn't see any point to it.

April 5 came, and Stephen and I drove to the department of motor vehicles and I took my driving test and passed it.

That night my mom made me a birthday dinner, followed by cake and ice cream. After the cake, Mom and Stephen told me to go look out in the driveway. I guess I was too old to be blindfolded. When I saw the birthday present, for one instant I felt like I was in our old backyard, seeing a brand-new BMX bike leaning up against the brick barbecue. Only this was a slightly used all-wheel-drive Jeep. Stephen had had somebody deliver it right to our driveway.

I drove it to school every day, and gave Fawn and Lyric and their teammates rides to practices and games, which took a lot of the burden off Mom and Stephen, and helped justify the credit card they let me use for gas.

I'd gotten what I wanted, but something definitely didn't feel right. I was a sixteen-year-old kid living in a McMansion with his own Jeep and credit card. Life was easy, school was easy. Anything this easy had to make you wary—there had to be something bad crouching in the shadows up ahead, waiting to pounce.

One evening in May—it was our tenth month of living in the new house—my mom and I were the only ones home. Mom poured herself a glass of wine and took a sip. She said, "Remember when we used to talk about how everything is just temporary, nothing lasts? Well, I think it's time to change that philosophy. I think we're into something long-term now, don't you, Milo? This is going to last."

It sounded nice, but I wasn't convinced. I thought, Show me anything in life that lasts or stays the same. No, I don't buy it. Everything changes. Everything.

But then it struck me: If everything changes, how could I possibly be the same old Milo? It didn't make sense.

# 24

wake–rouse–ignite–illuminate–reveal–
expose–uncover–find

That night I woke up suddenly at three a.m. in a tangle of sheets and blankets. I'd been having a wild dream, but the instant I woke up it tumbled out of my mind and I completely forgot what I'd been dreaming.

I was not only awake at three in the morning, I felt more awake and alert than I usually did during the day-time. My body felt as though a power cord had been plugged into me. Or like I was the power cord and I'd been plugged into something else.

I got up and went downstairs and bumped around in the dark, silent house, feeling my way past the shadowy shapes of furniture. I wandered into the living room, the least-used room in our house. The floor seemed spongy and bouncy to my feet. I kept trying to remember the dream

I'd been having, but it was gone. The only thing left was the vague feeling that something or somebody was waving to me.

I sat down on the couch in the living room and listened to the dead silence of the house. I could hear a clock ticking.

I looked around at the shadows and the colorless objects. Over by the fireplace was a bin full of old newspapers that we used for starting fires. There was just enough light leaking from somewhere, maybe from moonlight, for me to pick out a single word on the top newspaper. The longer I stared at that word, the more it looked like an odd, foreign word, just floating there.

TRAVEL

I reached over and turned on the lamp next to the couch. I had to squint for a moment at the sudden brightness. I knelt down to the newspaper bin and picked up the Travel section on top. The main article and photo were about Rio de Janeiro. I turned the page and scanned the ads. Turkey. Canada. Mexico. Hot Deals in Paradise. I had no idea what I was looking for, but I turned another page and continued. Victoria. Australia. Information on camel safaris. China.

Nothing seemed to jump out at me, and I tossed the paper back onto the bin. As I did that, I noticed a magazine-sized newspaper sticking out from the pile. It was one of the little neighborhood weekly newspapers that my mom used to read when we were living in Seattle. She still picked one up every once in a while—she liked to keep up on what was happening around the old neighborhoods.

I still had no idea what I was looking for, but I yanked it out from under the stack of papers and started flipping through it. I stopped when I came to a page called "What's Doing." It had a list of the week's events in the neighborhood, with the meeting places and times. The events were current—they were all happening this week in May. Senior square dancing . . . Home-buying seminar . . . Krafty Knitters . . . Saturday morning bird-watchers club . . . Jigsaw Puzzlers . . .

I was just about to toss the paper back into the bin and turn off the lamp when my eyes skimmed over one of the events, and my blood froze. My breath stopped.

**Slice of Swiss Cheese: My Travels Across Switzerland**
The Happy Travelers Society of Seattle hosts Valerie Swinford, who will give a mixed-media performance on traveling in Switzerland. Saturday 10 a.m. Borden Room, West Puget Community College campus. Free admission; wheelchair-accessible.

I held it up to the lamp and read it over and over.

• • •

Saturday morning my mom made me some breakfast while I studied the directions to West Puget Community College that I'd printed out.

"Okay, so, refresh my memory," she said. "You're going to be in Seattle all day?"

"Yeah."

"At a lecture?"

"Yeah."

"And this is for school?"

"No."

"You're going . . . with someone?"

"No."

"Are you meeting someone there?"

"No."

Fawn's voice called out from the other room, "Can you drop us off at the field on your way?"

"Yeah, be ready in ten minutes," I said.

Then, not knowing why I was blushing, I showed Mom the scrap of paper I'd torn out of the "What's Doing" page.

She put on her glasses and read it, and gasped.

"Oh my goodness, why didn't you say so? How interesting! Ms. Swinford! Oh, how strange. Are you going to say hello to her? Say hello to her for me. Find out everything you can. Find out the whole story."

"What whole story?" I said.

"You know. What happened. Why she got fired. I mean . . . you know, if the subject comes up."

# 25

auditorium–theater–performance–
entertainment–act–ham–butt–buttocks–
buttinsky

I sat down in the very last row of the auditorium and waited for Ms. Swinford to come out onstage.

The Borden Room looked like it could seat about three hundred people, but it was pretty empty—I counted only thirty-nine heads. I was the youngest person there. The other thirty-eight were mostly gray-haired grandmas and grandpas, a few old hippies with ponytails, and middle-aged women in twos and threes.

At ten a.m. a smiling, excited lady bounced up to the podium. She thanked all of us for coming, on behalf of the Happy Travelers Society. She asked us to donate some money on our way out so they could sponsor more fun, free events and special guests like the one we were about to enjoy this morning . . .

"And now, ladies and gentlemen, let us all please welcome . . . Valerie Swinford and her Slice of Swiss Cheese!"

The applause sounded thin and weak in the nearly empty auditorium.

A lady came out onto the stage. She was carrying her guitar and wearing a festive Swiss-looking skirt, like something out of *The Sound of Music.* Black nylons, colorful vest, and very low-cut blouse. She clipped the cordless mic to her vest and swung her guitar into position.

I was in shock.

It was Ms. Swinford, but she'd gotten younger!

"Good morning, everyone!" she said.

"Um-mm," the audience murmured.

(I remembered how all of us fifth graders used to reply in unison, "Good morning, Ms. Swinford.")

"How is everyone this morning? Happy to be here?"

"Um-mm."

(The class: "Yes, Ms. Swinford.")

She wasn't wearing glasses. She used to say she couldn't see a thing without them. And her hair was different. It used to be short and curly; now it was shoulder-length and straight and darker, and her bangs formed curtains over her eyes. Her cheeks hadn't changed—they were still as plump and apple-red as ever.

She had a nice rack.

Racks were not something I had noticed in fifth grade.

She started singing. She sang a jolly mountain tune from the Bavarian Alps. I remembered it from fifth grade. She followed it with more mountain songs, and every time I recognized one of them I got goose bumps.

The audience applauded dutifully after each song, but otherwise they just sat there like stumps. Like toppled dinosaurs.

Then she started to sing "The Happy Wanderer."

*I love to go a-wandering along the mountain track . . .*

I felt a lump forming in my throat. But something was happening up front; there was some kind of distraction. A side door opened and someone came into the auditorium. All heads turned to look. It was a tall girl with a pile of styled black hair and a shiny peach-colored rain slicker, which she took off before sitting down in the far right seat in the second row. She looked all around, beaming at the rest of the audience. I saw her profile, her long nose that sloped downward like this auditorium. Oh, Lord. It couldn't be. It was Penny Partnow.

What was she doing here?

Ms. Swinford didn't stop singing, but squinted over at Penny. Penny waved, but Ms. Swinford just kept singing and playing the guitar.

After two or three more songs, Ms. Swinford put her guitar down and woke up her sleeping laptop and started her PowerPoint show. She narrated each colorful slide projected on the screen behind her. She was in a lot of the pictures herself, wearing her old glittery cat's-eye glasses. These pictures were almost all familiar to me. Most of them were slides she used to show us in fifth grade. In the pictures, she looked exactly like the Ms. Swinford I remembered, not the one narrating them now.

There she was, sitting on a picturesque wooden bridge above the rushing Reuss River in Lucerne. There she was, posing beside a wood-carved bear in Bern. There was the shot of the little village of Zermatt, the "footstool of the Matterhorn." And there were Aunt Liesl and Uncle Cedric! Yes, it was them, standing in a sunny Alpine meadow with the Matterhorn in the background—the real Matterhorn! Uncle Cedric with his pencil-thin mustache and felt hat with a feather sticking out of it. Aunt Liesl's blond braids.

Ms. Swinford paused to take a sip of water from a bottle. I noticed that her hand trembled.

"You know," she said, "I used to be a teacher. In my past life. Until I got fired."

A few people in the audience tittered.

"That's right," she said. "I lasted only a year and a half. When I think of all that time and effort I invested, only to get the boot . . . I was devastated. See, I'd always believed my life was following a plan, a perfect divine plan. My happy childhood in Wenatchee, my travels across Switzerland, my opportunity to share my stories and experiences with my students. I just couldn't believe I could get fired."

She took another drink of water.

I wondered why she was saying all this. Was it part of her show?

"Well, I really hit bottom. For three and a half years I

wallowed in depression. I was too ashamed to go back to my hometown of Wenatchee. I got a job working in a bar as a cocktail waitress.

"And then one day about a year ago, I got out my old slides, and I looked at them again, just as you're seeing them right now. I remembered that wonderful year I spent in Switzerland. I remembered my fifth graders, especially some of the really special ones. I remembered what Aunt Liesl and Uncle Cedric used to say to me: 'Accept what happens without judgment. Look out at the world from the clear, sunny slopes of the Matterhorn. See the world from this higher perspective, and know that there are no boundaries, it's all one.' And suddenly I felt a sense of peace. I realized that my getting fired had to be part of the plan, and I must have been meant to perform and share in a different way. And here I am."

Ms. Swinford smiled out at the audience, all forty of us. There was dead silence, except for some old geezer snorting into a handkerchief. Then someone started clapping— oh my God, it was a *slow* clap. It was Penny Partnow. The rest of the audience joined in.

"Thank you, thank you," Ms. Swinford said. "Thank you so much. And now I'm going to put my glasses on and take some questions from the audience."

The glasses she put on were a plain, modern style, not the old glittery cat's-eyes.

"Ah, there you are!" she said, scanning the audience. "Hi, everybody. I'm blind without my glasses but I sing better to blurry faces. Sometimes there are so many old sour-pusses."

Penny waved again, and this time Ms. Swinford recognized her and let out a yelp and said, "Oh my God! Penny!" She beamed and waved at Penny with both her hands, and once again the whole audience craned their necks to look at Penny, wondering who the heck this girl was—daughter? sister?

The Q&A began. An ex-hippie raised his hand and wanted to know a good cheap place to stay in Geneva. Somebody asked about mule rides around Lake Lucerne. An old geezer wondered about the Swiss railroad system as compared to the German and Italian. Ms. Swinford answered every question briskly and efficiently, just like a professional travel guide.

There was a question from an elderly lady sitting by herself a couple rows in front of me—I had noticed her talking to herself earlier. She wanted to know if it was true that if she took her cat to Switzerland, the Swiss would kill it and eat it.

"Yes, that's still a common practice in Switzerland," Ms. Swinford said. "Next question?"

A woman wanted to hear more details about Ms. Swinford's year and a half as a fifth-grade teacher. Like why, for instance, did she get fired?

"Why did they fire me? They fired me because I shared too much of myself. I used to tell my students all about my life and my experiences and philosophies. I told them about Aunt Liesl and Uncle Cedric. I talked to them about spiritual things, our search for truth and beauty and enlightenment. About how we each need to find our own higher consciousness. Some of the kids understood me and others didn't. The ones who didn't went home and told their parents and made me sound crazy, and some of their parents came after me."

She hesitated, then smiled. "But I loved the fifth graders. God, I loved them! I loved them too much, that was my problem. I remember there were five or six truly memorable kids in my class my first year. They were my pets. Of course, a teacher isn't supposed to have pets. But they really were special. And there's one of them, sitting right there!"

Ms. Swinford extended her arm, palm up, in Penny's direction. Penny, for some bizarre reason, stood up and started waving to the audience, and the audience, for some even more bizarre reason, applauded, as if Penny were a celebrity. Sit your big fat butt down, I wanted to yell out. It was so typical Penny Partnow.

# 26

exit–opening–mouth–talk–hot air–
thermal–firestorm–bombshell–thunderbolt–
bolt from the blue

After the show, the audience filed toward the exits. A few people approached the stage to shake hands with Ms. Swinford. I could read her lips: "Thank you!" "Nice to meet you!"

I stayed in my seat. I wanted to wait for the place to clear out before I went up to Ms. Swinford myself.

But there was a problem. Penny had rushed to the stage. Now she and my former teacher were exchanging hugs and gleeful squeals.

I wasn't about to go down there and foist myself between the two of them. They were chatting away while Ms. Swinford packed up her guitar and laptop. Eventually they walked down the stage steps together, still talking nonstop as they went through the side door.

I got up and hurried down the carpeted auditorium steps. I went through the same door they'd just gone through and came outside into the concrete square. It was drizzling and the pavement was glazed. They were gone.

No, there they were. Walking stride for stride across the campus square, still absorbed in conversation. Ms. Swinford was carrying her black laptop bag. Penny was carrying Ms. Swinford's guitar case.

I followed them.

Everyone who passed them seemed to do a double take. Ms. Swinford in her Swiss outfit, Penny all mature and confident in her glossy rain slicker and long legs and tight corduroy pants, her big explosion of hair, and looking all the more artsy for carrying a guitar case.

They stopped at a small white car. Ms. Swinford opened the hatchback and Penny helped her load the stuff in. I lurked next to a tree.

They got in. The car started. Exhaust, taillights. The car backed out of the parking space.

I started to feel panicky.

*Do something, you idiot.*

Do what?

I didn't come here to see Penny Partnow. I didn't want to have to compete with her for Ms. Swinford's attention.

*But you don't have any choice. You're here. So move it.*

I dashed for the car as it was leaving the parking lot. I caught up to Penny's window and pounded on it.

Penny jumped about three feet.

The car stopped.

They peered at me through the fogged window.

Penny rolled it down.

She screamed. "Milo? It's Milo Bastion! Oh my God! Where did you come from?"

"Milo?" Ms. Swinford said, almost at the same time as Penny.

In fact, I think Ms. Swinford might have said it first.

• • •

They invited me to join them for a bite to eat.

"I just can't believe it. What a wonderful surprise," Ms. Swinford said, while Penny tried to tilt her seat forward so I could squeeze into the backseat. Such a talent and genius, yet she couldn't figure out how to slide the seat forward.

"My two all-time favorite students in the whole world. Did you both catch my show? Wasn't it a trip? What a dead audience. What a bunch of corpses. I need a drink. I know a place a few blocks away."

When I'd finally crawled into the backseat and sat up, my field of vision was completely blocked by Penny's dampened hair.

"I can't wait to hear all about you guys," Ms. Swinford said.

"I just finished shooting another TV commercial," Penny said.

"A TV commercial, really? My goodness! I can't wait to

hear about it. I can't wait to hear *both* your stories. But first I just want to find that place . . ."

She turned down another street. As she was driving, she took out a cigarette and lit it up. Penny swung her face around and looked at her with horror. I was shocked, too, but I tried not to show it.

"I didn't know you were a smoker," Penny said.

Ms. Swinford lowered her window halfway and blew the smoke out.

"It does sort of bother my eyes, not to mention gets all in my clothes and hair," Penny said.

"Roll your window down," Ms. Swinford said.

"Yeah, right." Penny laughed. "And fill my lungs with bus fumes!"

Ms. Swinford drove up the avenue, smoking. Suddenly she hit the brakes and swerved into an empty space at the curb. We climbed out. She led us up the street to a café. The sign said THE DISABLED CAFÉ. She dropped her cigarette on the sidewalk and ground it with her pointy black shoe. The shoe had a square buckle on it. Her black nylons went up and disappeared under her Swiss skirt.

We went inside the café and sat down at a round table next to a window. The window looked out at the wet sidewalk and the mashed cigarette. Raindrops chased each other down the glass.

"You guys order anything you want. My treat," Ms. Swinford said. She ordered a draft beer, the darkest on tap.

Penny asked for tea in a pot, but they only had it in mugs. I went for a cup of coffee.

The place was buzzing with conversation. It seemed to be filled with locals. Penny took off her rain slicker, looked around all perky for a place to hang it, and ended up folding it over another chair.

She gave her bright turquoise neck scarf a little tug. The color was obviously chosen to go with her tanned complexion and brown eyes.

"Cute place," Penny said. "Disabled Café. Did you know that if you take the two *d*'s off *disabled*, you get 'is able'?"

Ms. Swinford reached down into her bag and took out another cigarette.

"Sorry to say it's against the law to smoke in public places," Penny said.

"Oh. Yeah," Ms. Swinford said. "I keep forgetting." She dropped the cigarette into her bag.

I couldn't help taking a long healthy look down her low-cut blouse.

"Now then, you two," she said, "now that I have you here together. Let's catch up and find out what we've all been up to the last five years, shall we?"

"I'm president of the regional chapter of Teen Fellowship," Penny said. "And I already mentioned the Tasty-Stix commercial. Let's see, what else? Gosh . . . I've done fashion modeling for some local retail stores, very high-end stuff. I've appeared in two sing-along videos for tots. I teach modern jazz dance to a group of hearing-impaired middle schoolers. Oh, gosh, let's see, what else . . ."

"My, my," Ms. Swinford said. "Very impressive, Penny. We always knew you'd be president of something some-day."

The waitress came with our beverages. When Penny paused, Ms. Swinford raised her mug of dark beer and said, "To all our exciting journeys."

"My journey really has been one huge adventure," Penny said. "Many, many trophies, plaques, ribbons, awards. As you may remember, I've been keeping a daily journal-slash-diary since I was five. The theme of my first sixteen years is how I've kept myself open to new, exciting adventures waiting up ahead, around the next corner. Just like you used to tell us."

"Yes, indeed," Ms. Swinford said. She yawned. Her eyes watered. "Oh, my. That was a long morning."

"I know what you mean," Penny said, still dunking her tea bag up and down in her mug. "Don't you just find performing exhilarating but also exhausting? Don't you just *love* doing a show? But we're always performing, aren't we? I mean, yes, I'm an actress. Yes, I'm a dancer. Yes, I'm president of the regional chapter of Teen Fellowship. I'm an A student at a progressive charter school. But they're just roles. Hi, there! How are you? Oh, I thought those people over there knew me. Oops. They were looking at me like they recognized me."

"I'll bet that happens to you a lot," Ms. Swinford said.

"Penny, you know I love you, but you do go on. Let's hear from Milo now."

"Yeah, let's hear from Milo," Penny said agreeably. "Hey, Milo, remember that potluck you had at your house? Remember how hot it was that day? I'll bet you can't remember what I was wearing that day."

"The potluck," Ms. Swinford said, smiling. "I remember that."

They both looked at me.

What?

They seemed to be studying me.

I could feel my face blush. I took a gulp of coffee.

"He's not going to speak," Penny said.

"I don't remember him as being shy," Ms. Swinford said. "You used to be very talkative, Milo."

They continued to observe me.

"He became a man of few words when he moved away," Penny said. "I wrote him tons of letters and he never once wrote back to me."

"Not tons," I said. My voice came out strained.

"Okay, whatever," Penny said. "Valerie, I have a great idea," she said, leaning close to Ms. Swinford. "I wanted to ask you if you'd come and be our featured guest at Teen Fellowship one night. You can do your show for us. We can't pay you very much, I'm afraid. Like barely anything. But it'll be a great audience. Everybody will love your show. They'll *get* it."

"You think so?"

"Absolutely. Those old folks today, they're the wrong audience for you. You need to perform for young people. You'll be a hit at Teen Fellowship. Your act is so funky-retro it's actually cool. What do you say?"

Ms. Swinford smiled. "All right. I'd love to."

"Great!"

I looked out the window. There was some blue sky directly overhead, but black mountains of clouds were forming.

I was thinking I had made a mistake in coming here. I had felt such a need to reconnect with Ms. Swinford, but I was too tight, and time was running out and it was starting to look like nothing magical or monumental was going to happen.

"Did I mention I've been keeping a daily journal-slash-diary since I was five?" Penny said. "I'm getting ready to—"

"Yeah, you mentioned it," I said. "Journal-slash-diary. Yeah, we got it."

Penny gave me a look. Ms. Swinford laughed.

"I'm going to write it up," Penny went on. "The first volume of my memoirs. The first sixteen years. The theme will be my search for truth, beauty, and perfection. Or truth, beauty, and me. I just want to spread myself around."

You spread it around all right, I thought.

Ms. Swinford said, "I've always liked the fact that you're your favorite person in the world, Penny. I think there's something genuine about that. Something childlike. You are also one of *my* favorite people."

"Really? What a nice thing to say, Valerie. Do you really mean it?"

"I do. Oh, it's true that you have a hard time being quiet, but I don't know if that's a criticism. It's just you. Just the way you are."

I looked out the window some more. I should just leave. Let these two have their lovefest together. I couldn't even imagine calling Ms. Swinford "Valerie." It seemed too grownup for me.

Penny was saying, "Now that I'm regional president of Teen Fellowship, one of my missions is really to *listen* more and talk less and . . ."

I tuned her out. Through the window, I saw that the black clouds had completely taken over the sky. It started pouring rain. The wind came in gusts. People were rushing by on the sidewalk. Every time somebody opened the door of the café, in came a whoosh of outdoors.

When I looked at Ms. Swinford again, I saw that she was looking at me.

"What're you thinking, Milo?" she asked.

Penny was still talking, but when she realized Ms. Swinford wasn't listening to her, her voice trailed off into silence.

I said, "I was just wondering . . . You're not a teacher anymore?"

"That's right."

"Do you do a lot of these shows?" I asked.

"You mean like this morning? No, not really. I'd like to do more, but there's not much demand."

"And don't forget I'm going to book you for Teen Fellowship."

"That's right, Penny," Ms. Swinford said. "And I'm doing Bumbershoot this year."

"Bumbershoot! Oh my God, that's a major festival," Penny said. "That's a big gig for you, Valerie. I will just have to mark that one on my calendar, for sure."

"What do you do for a living?" I asked Ms. Swinford.

"I work in a club up in Marysville."

"A club?"

"Yeah, it's actually a small casino and card room next to an Indian reservation. Men go there to drink and play poker and watch some entertainment. I'm the entertainment."

"How cool," Penny said. "You sing and play guitar?"

"I strip. I'm a topless dancer."

I had to grip the table to keep from falling out of my chair.

Penny had a frozen smile. She gave her turquoise neck scarf a little tug. Finally she said brightly, "Well, that's . . . an art form."

"It pays the bills."

"And it sure keeps you fit," Penny said. "When I think about it, I'd rather get paid to dance naked than sit in some office all day."

"That's kind of how I see it," Ms. Swinford said.

"How about your social life?" Penny asked. "Anyone special?"

Ms. Swinford shook her head. "No, I'm alone. There's no one."

"Did you ever go back to Switzerland?" I asked. "Whatever happened to Aunt Liesl and Uncle Cedric? Are you ever going back again?"

Ms. Swinford looked puzzled. She turned to Penny. "I thought you told him?"

"No."

"You never told him? I just assumed you had. I told you you could. The last time I saw you, at the potluck. You asked if you could tell him, and I said yes, go ahead."

"Tell me what?" I said.

"Well, I didn't tell him," Penny said. "I would have, but he never gave me the chance. Like I said, he never wrote back, so I said to myself, Well, if he's not even going to write me back, then I won't bother to tell him."

"Tell me what?" I said again.

They both looked at me, and then at each other.

Outside there was a loud boom of thunder. And then a flash of lightning. It was like a horror movie. The boom reverberated for many seconds and shook the windows. Conversations in the café stopped all at once, as if everyone were holding his breath.

The rain came down in torrents. Cars slowed to a crawl. It was dark outside.

The lights in the café flickered and went off.

Then they came back on.

"My goodness." Ms. Swinford held up her empty beer glass. "I could go for another one of these. How about you guys? Refills?"

# 27

refill–restore–correct–divulge–confess–
disclose–unmask–bare–strip–cast off

Ms. Swinford had gotten her refill, I had fresh coffee, and Penny had another cup of tea.

It was harder for me to look at Ms. Swinford now that I knew she was a topless dancer. I had to concentrate on her from the chin up.

"Okay, here's my confession," she said. "It was all a lie."

"You're not really a topless dancer?" I said. My eyes dropped uncontrollably to her blouse. I took a swig of coffee.

"No, not that," Ms. Swinford said. "My whole act, my stories, everything. It was all fake. All my stories about life on the farm with my big happy family in Wenatchee? It was all made up. My life in Wenatchee was hell. I never knew my father. My mother kicked me out when I was fifteen. I've never been to Switzerland in my life. I've never even been out of Washington State."

"What?"

"I made it all up."

"What about . . . what about the cuckoo clock?"

"It's not that tough to buy a Swiss cuckoo clock without going to Switzerland."

"But all those slides and photos of Switzerland. You're *in* some of those pictures."

"I just used a very advanced photo-editing tool on my computer. They're all authentic pictures of Switzerland; I inserted myself into them. They're very good, aren't they? I take a lot of pride in that work. In some ways I enjoy those fake pictures more than if I had taken them myself for real. Nobody ever noticed. Nobody except Penny. She nailed me halfway through the fifth-grade year."

"And I probably never would have noticed either, if it hadn't been for a few very obvious blunders," Penny said. "Like when she told us the Matterhorn was on the Swiss-German border. I'm like, excuse me. The Matterhorn is on the Swiss-Italian border, not the Swiss-German. I mean, I knew *that* when I was in kindergarten. And she told us the word *Matter* in Matterhorn means 'Mother.' She totally made that up."

"I made everything up," Ms. Swinford said. "At first I didn't even care if half of it was wrong. But when Penny started calling me on it—in private, fortunately—I had to go and check my facts and do a little more research for authenticity. But Penny can keep her mouth shut when she gives her word. She never told anybody, bless her heart. Apparently not even you, Milo."

"You made it all up? You made up Switzerland?"

"Well, I mean, there is an actual country."

"Where did you get all the photos?"

"CD-ROMs, shareware, Web sites."

"But why did you make it all up in the first place? Why did you lie?"

"I didn't see it as lying. I saw it as exercising my imagination. Making fiction. I loved it. I loved that it existed in my imagination. I had created a whole myth around myself. My very own myth. Even to this day, when I do a show I just make up anything I want. The challenge is to make it sound convincing. Mostly I stick to the facts, but occasionally I let my imagination go a little crazy."

"Like today," Penny said. "I couldn't believe it when that lady in the audience asked you if the Swiss would kill and eat her cat and you said yes. Nobody even called you on it. It was so absurd, it was kind of a beautiful moment, in a way."

"I thought it sounded a little strange," I said. "But you seemed like such an expert."

"That's the beauty of it," Ms. Swinford said. "The utter insanity of it. People want so much to have experts to believe in. That's the fun."

"In fifth grade I believed everything you told us," I said. "I believed in you."

"Oh, what does that mean, 'believed in me'? You believed my *stories*, you didn't believe in *me*. And I don't think it ruined your life, did it?"

"Why did you have to make it all up and lie to us? Why did you tell all those happy stories about Wenatchee?"

"Because it made everybody feel good. What, you'd rather I told about all the depressing garbage?"

"So you made up a whole fake childhood with fake parents and brothers and sisters."

"That's right."

"But what about Switzerland? Why couldn't you just be honest and say you'd never been there but you wanted to go someday?"

"It wouldn't have been as much fun. I wouldn't have been an expert. It was more fun to pretend and make up my own stuff and entertain people instead of having to stick to boring old facts."

"And you," I said, turning to Penny. "You didn't tell anybody? I can't believe that."

"You can't believe I could keep my mouth shut? I don't blame you there. But Valerie wasn't hurting anybody. What kind of satisfaction would I have gotten from blowing the whistle on her? I would only have hurt her. I loved her. She got me through fifth grade. She got *you* through fifth grade, Milo. And part of it was because of all the good things she told us."

"All the lies she told us. This is bizarre," I said, wiping my forehead. "This is totally bizarre. You're crazy." I looked at Ms. Swinford. "You lied to a bunch of fifth graders who trusted you. You lie every time you show that slide show and tell all those stories."

"Well." Ms. Swinford seemed stymied for a moment. "I mean, they *were* real photographs, even though I didn't take them."

"What about Aunt Liesl and Uncle Cedric?" I asked.

"I made them up."

"Who were those people in the pictures?"

"Photos from an online encyclopedia."

I sank my face into my hands. I felt like a royal sucker. What a fool. Beyond anything else, I was embarrassed. Embarrassed, humiliated. Tricked. Deceived. Duped. What other synonyms could I think of?

I felt Ms. Swinford's hand on my arm.

"You okay?"

"I'm okay, I'm okay," I said into my hands. "I don't need to go to the nurse's office."

She laughed. "What?"

It felt comfortable keeping my hands over my face. The equivalent of hiding under the sheets. Making the world go away.

I muttered into my hands, "You asked me once if I needed to go to the nurse's office."

"I did?"

"We were singing 'The Happy Wanderer.' I went running out of the classroom and—"

"Oh, yes, yes," Ms. Swinford said. "I remember. Yes."

"So do I," Penny said. But she didn't say it in her know-it-all regional president of Teen Fellowship voice.

I pulled my hands away and blinked a few times. Everything was smudged for a moment. Penny's face came into focus. I remembered the look on her face that day, the day I rushed out of the room.

I said to Ms. Swinford, "I went out into the hall. You came out and asked me if I wanted to go to the nurse's office. I said no. So you took me in that room and gave me some tissues."

"Yes, I remember," Ms. Swinford said. "I remember it all."

"That synonym book was the only thing that was real," I said.

"The what?" Ms. Swinford said.

"The synonym book. We played with a synonym book."

"I don't remember that. I just wanted to help."

"You took advantage—you jerked everybody around," I said. "A bunch of gullible fifth graders. We would've fallen for anything you told us. But you didn't believe any of it."

"That's not exactly true," Ms. Swinford said. "I believed it. I knew it wasn't true, but I still believed it. I wanted to make it real to *you*. That's what a storyteller does. Makes it come alive."

"You guys, this is so cool," Penny said. "This is *exactly* the kind of stuff we talk about at Teen Fellowship."

"What stuff?" Ms. Swinford said.

"Like what's real and what's illusion. Like what people get fooled by. That's why I was trying to get you to come to Teen Fellowship, Milo. We talk about this stuff every week."

"I don't want to talk about it," I said. "It's all crap. It's all make-believe."

I stood up and put on my jacket.

"Tell me what isn't make-believe," Ms. Swinford said. "Milo, you don't have anything to be embarrassed about. All right, so you've spent the past few years believing in something that wasn't true. Did it help or not? If it helped you, then what difference does it make whether it was real or make-believe? You should use whatever you can to get you through the day. Sit down. Sit down and let's have some pie."

I stood there and imagined myself looking very cool and walking out of the restaurant. Not saying another word, just walking out. Finally, my chance to make a dignified exit.

I'd be walking out on a liar. That's all she was. Maybe she had meant well, maybe she had even loved us, but she was a liar. You couldn't go around making up anything you wanted just for the hell of it or to make people feel good. The truth meant something. It had to be worth something, whether it made people feel happy or sad.

Outside the window the rain had stopped. Steam was rising from the pavement. I looked back at Ms. Swinford. Was she crazy? How could she not be? All the stories about Wenatchee. All the hours she'd spent laboring over JPEG files on a computer screen, cropping and pasting images of herself onto digital photos of Switzerland. Making up a couple of characters like Aunt Liesl and Uncle Cedric. She was a whack job!

A royal whack job.

And yet I'd been carrying Ms. Swinford around with me for the past five years. She'd loved us. I had known it in fifth grade; I'd felt it. That's what I'd carried around with me for five years. There must have been truth in that.

What if I'd never had her as my teacher? What if I'd had one of the other fifth-grade teachers at our school? Would I have been any different? What if my parents had won the lottery or we'd used that brick barbecue just once?

Some things in life you could choose—the rules you obeyed, the most precise words, things like that. But you couldn't choose who came and went in your life. Things came and went; there was nothing solid about it.

I listened. The conversations in the café seemed to blend into one steady noise.

Then I saw something very strange. Outside, a fine mist was falling. It seemed to be coming from nowhere. It was like being up in the mountains, in the middle of clouds.

It was all just mist. My past, my whole story. Mist and myth.

The tightness I'd been carrying around inside me all day seemed to let go. The air seemed thinner, and I felt myself breathe easily. I felt myself smiling. I could practically feel the cool mist in my face. Penny and Ms. Swinford were watching me. I must have had a goofy grin on, because they both burst out laughing. I started laughing, too. I fell back into my chair. People were looking at us. We ordered some pie.

# 28

summer–sunny–pleasant–enchanted–
bewitched–cursed–damned–doomed–fate–
destiny

My tenth-grade year ended and summer started. Mom and I took another camping trip together. She liked being a stay-at-home mom and she seemed to like having me around the house. But I still felt kind of guilty that I had this stuff—Jeep, credit card, private bathroom. What had I really done to deserve any of it? I went and got a summer job delivering pizzas. Might as well start amassing my fortune.

I still thought a lot about Ms. Swinford, but I didn't wonder who was the real Ms. Swinford and who was the make-believe one. There were two Ms. Swinfords—the one at the Disabled Café and the one I'd known in fifth grade.

One gorgeous day that summer I was in the mood for a drive, so I headed southeast toward Kangley to pay a visit to the old Bon Repos. I left in the early morning on a Tuesday. When I finally made it to the Bon Repos, I could barely tell the difference between the Phases. I couldn't tell where the woods used to be. The Phases had all blended together. So had the people. There was one big planet Bon Repos.

I couldn't even find Jastin Spitters's apartment, though I didn't try too hard. I knew he was probably in jail. It sounded corny for me to think that he had embraced the dark side, but that was how I thought of him.

I was hungry, so I drove out of the complex to the nearest strip mall that had a deli. I parked and got out. The sun was starting to bake the chewing gum on the sidewalk. A couple of doors from the deli, I passed some sort of martial arts studio. There was a class going on inside, eight people, all women, stretching on the mat. The sign on the window said MASTER RON'S TAE KWON DO. Underneath was another sign that read: THE JOURNEY OF DISCIPLINE, CONCENTRATION, INNER STRENGTH, AND HARMONY.

I looked at my reflection in the glass. For a second, I wasn't even sure whose face it was. A high school pizza delivery boy's.

Why hadn't I started my own journey of discipline, concentration, inner strength, and harmony? Where was my rite of passage? What did it take to start? How did you jump in?

I noticed some photos in the window, along with some tae kwon do trophies on display. There were pictures of Master Ron and his students. He was standing with a team of students who had won awards in a tournament back in June. They were wearing white tae kwon do outfits and holding up their medals. One of the students in the picture was Jastin Spitters. I leaned closer to the glass. It was him, all right. The same dark arched eyebrows. The same face.

I thought, That's something that never changes: a person's face.

He was smiling and holding a silver medal. I looked back at my own face, or rather at the reflection of it, and it was grinning.

# 29

ad-message-communication-conversation-
exchange-transfer-bequeath-hand down-
deliver-let go-liberate

At the end of August I started seeing a lot of ads for Bumbershoot. I wanted to go and watch Ms. Swinford perform there.

So I phoned Penny and asked her if she'd go with me. She seemed surprised I'd called, and she didn't answer right away. And I thought, Here's her perfect opportunity to get me back for all the times I was mean to her. She's been waiting for the chance, pretending to be nice, just waiting for this moment to get revenge.

I decided to beat her to the punch. I said, "Before you answer, I just want to apologize." And I told her what I was apologizing for. And how I wished I could undo it all and go back to fifth grade and— Well, no, not go back to fifth grade. But start over.

She said she'd love to.

"Which one?" I said. "Go to Bumbershoot or start over?"

On Labor Day I drove over to her house and picked her up. I was shocked at how run-down and neglected her house was on the outside. It might have been a commune, but apparently no one did any work on it. It needed some major painting and landscaping. It was hard to imagine her living there, even more so as she came walking out from it all neatly dressed in a stylish outfit. She didn't seem embarrassed or even aware of where she lived.

I had never been to Bumbershoot before. It ran all Labor Day weekend at the Seattle Center, live music nonstop on a dozen different stages. There were packs of drummers by the fountain and street entertainers every few feet with their own circles of watchers. There was food everywhere.

Ms. Swinford was scheduled to be performing in the Orca Room at eleven. It took us a lot of searching and walking around to find the Orca Room, but we finally found it.

The act before Ms. Swinford's was a lady playing a dulcimer and chanting about global warming. There were about fifty people in the audience, some sitting in metal folding chairs and some standing. Penny and I stood against the wall: The lady with the dulcimer closed her eyes and looked up to the ceiling and held out her hands to bless us. And I thought, If a lady with a dulcimer wants to bless me, I'll take it.

When her act was finished there was a short break, and some of the audience left while others arrived. Somebody was always coming or going. Penny and I found a couple of chairs and sat down. We talked while we waited for Ms. Swinford's act. Penny said she was no longer sure she wanted to be an actress. She said she wanted to travel someday. She asked me if I had many friends. I said, "Nah, I'm not too good at networking. I'm kind of a loner."

"I'm about as un-loner as you can get, but I don't have friends either," she said. "I drive everybody nuts. I talk and brag about myself so much. I always feel like I have to sell myself."

I was kind of surprised at this honesty. It hadn't really occurred to me that Penny might actually be *aware* that she drove people nuts, but just couldn't help herself.

When Ms. Swinford came out onstage with her guitar and laptop, she said, "Good morning, everybody!"

"Um-mm," the crowd said.

"Good morning, Ms. Swinford," I said under my breath.

"Happy to be here?" Ms. Swinford asked.

• • •

After the show Penny and I went backstage to say hello. Backstage was actually just over behind a screen next to the fire exit. Ms. Swinford was wearing the same costume as the last time I'd seen her. She seemed happy to see us. She said she couldn't wait for the Teen Fellowship gig in October.

After we said goodbye to her, Penny and I went out into the Bumbershoot crowd and spent the whole afternoon taking it all in. While we were watching some Gaelic dancers in kilts doing jigs on crossed swords, we ran into my father. It was a surprising moment. Dad seemed delighted. "Well, for heaven's sake! Milo! My gosh, what a surprise!"

We hugged each other and then I introduced him to Penny. He said his lady friend, Michelle, was waiting at a table for him with a bottle of wine and some friends. But they could wait. Dad wanted to know if I'd like to take a few minutes to talk. I told him that would be good, and Penny and I agreed to meet back at that spot in about an hour.

So Dad and I went walking off away from the crowds, where it was quieter. We walked along a path that went by a tall statue of a World War I doughboy.

"How's it going with the new stepfamily?" Dad asked.

"Oh, all right. It takes some getting used to."

"But you're feeling pretty happy there?"

"It's not real stressful or anything," I said.

"Good. Life can be stressful. Stress itself isn't a bad thing—it helps us learn and accomplish all sorts of things. But it shouldn't be stressful at home. Home should be a stress-free zone."

"Do you live up here now?" I asked Dad.

"Up here . . . You mean in Washington State? Michelle has some property on Vashon Island—you know, in Puget Sound. She has a boat—a nice-sized boat, a sixty-one-footer. We're going to take it up to Alaska—actually, we're leaving this Thursday."

"Wow, that sounds pretty cool," I said. "Going up to Alaska on your own boat."

"Yes. Yes."

It really did sound like fun to me. What a way to escape.

We both looked up at the statue.

I asked Dad how his work with the Cog was progressing.

Dad smiled and shook his head slowly. "Fool's gold," he said.

"Fool's gold?"

"Fool's gold. The Cog was fool's gold. It led me down a false trail."

I shook my head. "That's too bad. So now you're moving on to something else?"

Dad looked at me for a moment and then said, "Yes, of course I'm moving on to something else. That's all there is. I'll let you in on a little secret. The pleasure is all in the seeking and not in the finding."

He said it as if it were the most obvious thing in the world.

Strange, I had always thought the pleasure was in the having. But I understood what he was saying. I knew I was going to remember it for the rest of my life. It was my dad's gift to me. I think it's called a bequest—it's what he handed down to me, my inheritance. I saw my parents, saw them clearly, both my mom and my dad. I saw how they were both a part of me and I was a part of them, but I was myself, too.

"Dad, I need to tell you something. I hope it won't sound like I'm a victim or anything."

"Go ahead, I'm listening."

"When you left back in fifth grade, I felt like I lost a big chunk of myself. I missed you pretty bad. And then—I never heard a thing from you after Arizona. That was kind of painful. But I don't hold that against you. I don't blame you for anything. You're not responsible for my life. My life is all mine. I wish you well, Dad. I hope you have a really cool life."

"Well, thanks, Milo."

"Dad, do you mind if I make an observation?"

"Not at all."

"Well, you're kind of looking for yourself—we all are. But you always seem to be, well, kind of hooked up with a lady friend. Getting together and splitting up. It just seems like it'd take a lot of energy. I don't see how you can find yourself if you're using up all that energy on women. I don't know. It's just an observation."

Dad had a strange look on his face. He didn't say anything, but he seemed to be thinking about what I'd just said. Finally he nodded.

A short time after that, we said goodbye. I watched his back until he disappeared into the crowd.

I walked around Bumbershoot by myself for a while. I wanted to think. I needed to think of something that

I could trust. Something that wasn't fool's gold. I wished I could trust myself, but I knew that wasn't the answer. I knew I could never completely trust myself any more than I could completely trust someone else. I didn't want to make up a myth about myself either, the way Ms. Swinford had done. I wasn't going to sacrifice the truth. All I could do, all I can do, is look at life, at the mystery. Stop waiting for things to come and go. Jump in.

I spotted Penny a few yards away. She was standing in a crowd of people watching a street performer try to escape from a straitjacket. He kicked and twisted and thrashed on the pavement to try to loosen the straitjacket. The sun shone on the pavement. What a glorious day. Plenty of day left. Tomorrow I would start eleventh grade. Football practices five days a week. I didn't want to think about that right now. I moved into the middle of the crowd and linked my arm through Penny's and we watched the guy struggling to get himself out of the straitjacket, and when he finally got free we all cheered.